ISABEL FEENEY,
STAR REPORTER

ISABEL FEENEY,
STAR REPORTER

By Beth Fantaskey

Houghton Mifflin Harcourt

Boston New York

www.hmhco.com

The text was set in Dante MT Std.
Book design by Susanna Vagt

Library of Congress Cataloging-in-Publication Data
Fantaskey, Beth.
Isabel Feeney, star reporter / by Beth Fantaskey.
p. cm.
Summary: In the 1920s, a ten-year-old newsgirl who aspires to be a reporter at the Chicago Tribune investigates the murder of a gangster.
ISBN 978-0-544-58249-1
[1. Mystery and detective stories. 2. Reporters and reporting—Fiction. 3. Newspapers—Fiction. 4. Gangsters—Fiction. 5. Chicago (Ill.)— History—20th century—Fiction.] I. Title.
PZ7.F2222851S 2016
[Fic]—dc23
2014048445

Manufactured in the United States of America
DOC 10 9 8 7 6 5 4 3 2
4500587832

ISABEL FEENEY,
STAR REPORTER

CHAPTER 1

MURDER ON HALSTED STREET!" I HOLLERED, WAVING A fat copy of the *Chicago Tribune* in front of the last few people hurrying home for dinner, their heads bent against a wickedly cold wind. The streets were dark and dusted with snow, and I knew nobody was going to stop, but I had to sell as many newspapers as possible, so I kept trying. "Read all about it!"

The truth was, though, murder wasn't big news in my city. It seemed like somebody — usually a gangster — got killed pretty much every day. People could hardly be bothered to read about a homicide in Chicago in 1926. Even ladies were carrying guns — and using them. A whole part of the county jail, called Murderess's Row, was set aside for women who'd done somebody in.

"It's Prohibition," my mother always said with a sigh. "That law has made the city crazy!"

I didn't know much about laws, but I knew when to give up peddling papers. Setting my unsold copies on the sidewalk under a streetlamp, I used my teeth to yank off my dad's old wool gloves, dug into my pockets, and counted my meager profits.

Nine lousy cents!

Then I glanced at the pile of papers at my feet, checking to see who had written the murder story on the front page, and sure enough, I saw the name Maude Collier. I bet *she* got paid a lot to write news. Just like I would when I was a famous girl reporter, which *would* happen. I wouldn't be a stupid newsgirl forever. Maybe I'd even go to school again, someday . . .

"Isabel! Isabel Feeney!"

The sound of someone calling my name interrupted my daydream, and I looked up to see one of my regular customers, a pretty young lady named Colette Giddings, hurrying toward me. She was smiling and waving a fist that I knew held coins.

"Hey, Miss Giddings," I greeted her. She wore a fancy white fur coat instead of her usual wool one, so I added, "You look really nice tonight."

"Why, thank you, Isabel," she said, handing me some money. More money than the paper cost. Miss Giddings was just a clerk at the big department store, Marshall Field's, but she never asked for change. Then she frowned at me, concern in her wide brown movie-star eyes. Honestly, with her dark curly hair and her sweet smile, Miss Giddings could've gone to Hollywood and been an actress like Mary Pickford. Why couldn't I ever get my mousy brown curls to look that nice? "Where are your mittens, Isabel?" she demanded. "Your hands are turning blue!"

I'd jammed my gloves into my pocket, and I pulled them out to show her. "I've got these. They used to be my dad's, but with the fingers cut halfway off, they work okay."

"Oh, Isabel . . ." Miss Giddings's frown deepened. She knew all about how my father had died in the Great War, and the few times I'd mentioned him, it always made her sad. Then I'd wish I hadn't done it. "Here." She tucked her newspaper under her arm and started to remove her own leather gloves. "These will fit you better. I have another pair at home."

"I am not taking those!" I cried, my fair, freckled cheeks getting warm in spite of the cold wind. She held out the gloves, and I stepped back. "I won't!"

Miss Giddings opened her mouth to protest. Then she stopped herself, folded her gloves away in her purse, and apologized quietly. "I'm sorry, Izzie. I just worry about you, working out here in the cold. You know, having a son your age, I have a soft spot . . ."

I didn't know much about Miss Giddings's personal life, but she had mentioned her kid, Robert, before.

How come he was never with her?

And where was her husband?

Had he died in a trench in France, like my dad? Because the war had taken a lot of men.

I didn't feel like I could ask. And I didn't want her charity. "My mother will probably get me some mittens soon," I fibbed. "She's got a new job, cleaning a hospital at night."

Well, the part about the job was true. But it wasn't going to buy new mittens. I just hoped we could heat the house a little better.

"All right, Isabel," Miss Giddings said—still sounding worried. "You just be careful out here." Then she glanced down the street and suddenly seemed distracted. "I've got to run now, Izzie. Take care, okay?"

"Yeah, you too," I said, watching as she hurried away, toward whatever—or whoever—had caught her attention.

That was when I realized a man was waiting for her a few yards down the street. A tall guy who stood in the shadows, his hat pulled low and his hands jammed into the pockets of a long overcoat. When they met up, he took Miss Giddings's arm, and at first I was happy for her. She was a good person, and if her husband had been killed, it would be nice if she met somebody new.

A moment later, I wasn't so sure about that, because Miss Giddings and her friend were obviously arguing —though I couldn't hear what they said—and the man was rough with her as they walked into the darkness. He tugged at her fur coat, and she wobbled on heels that were higher than her usual shoes.

I kept staring even after Miss Giddings and the man

turned a corner. Then, because I couldn't exactly interfere in a spat between two adults, I bent to pick up my
stack of papers before the rising wind blew them away.
But that winter wind, as strong as it was, couldn't drown
out the sound of a gunshot. A single, sharp report that
echoed from the alley into which Miss Giddings and that
man had just disappeared.

No. I'd be able to hear *that* for the rest of my life.

CHAPTER 2

PROBABLY SHOULDN'T HAVE RUN *TOWARD* A GUNSHOT, BUT Miss Giddings always looked after me, if only by buying a paper she probably didn't even want, and I couldn't seem to stop my feet. They just kept flying toward that alley. And as I skidded around the corner, I was ready to scream at the guy in the overcoat, telling him to leave Miss Giddings alone, even though I had a bad feeling it was way too late for that.

But when I practically stumbled over the two of them, huddled in a heap by some barrels full of garbage, my warning turned to a . . . *what?*

Because it wasn't Miss Giddings lying stretched out on the snow, bleeding. It was the man in the overcoat.

Miss Giddings was kneeling over him, and when she turned her face to me, I could see by the moonlight that she was scared and confused, as if she didn't know what had just gone wrong. Our eyes met, and it seemed like she was asking me, a kid who hadn't seen anything, *What just happened?*

I also noticed, lying right next to her knees—her nice clothes were going to be a mess—a black object.

"Miss Giddings?" I ventured uncertainly. "Where did that *gun* come from?"

CHAPTER 3

S HE DIDN'T ANSWER MY QUESTION, AND I MOVED CLOSER to her, real slowly. In her white fur, wide-eyed and crouched down, she looked like a cat that might run away if I made a sudden move. "What happened?" I asked, glancing at the man, who was very still. His hat was a few feet away, in the middle of the alley, and there was a puddle of blood near his ear. Then I looked away, not wanting to see more, and met Miss Giddings's eyes again. "Is he . . ."

I couldn't seem to say *dead*. But she knew what I meant, and she nodded.

"Yes," she said softly. I barely heard her, because there were sirens blaring now, getting louder. Somebody must've called the police. Miss Giddings turned her face away from me, and her hand shook when she rested it on the dead man's shoulder. Aside from the missing hat, his clothes looked perfect, as if he might stand up and tell us both it was all a joke. But when I dared to look at his face —the *blood*—a second time . . .

"What happened?" I asked again, forcing myself to move closer and kneel down too. I'd never been that close to a dead person. Hadn't even seen my father's body, because he'd been buried in Europe, "with honors." At least that's what everybody told me, probably so I wouldn't feel bad knowing he was really in a trench somewhere, forgotten. I focused on the man's chest, not wanting to look into his eyes, and asked, "Who shot him?"

She didn't answer that question, either. She was staring past me, toward a car that was screeching to a halt, blocking the alley, and suddenly I felt kind of trapped. I also realized, for the first time, that there might very well be a killer still wandering around the alley. In all the excitement, I hadn't even thought of that.

As headlights from the police car caught me and Miss Giddings huddled like rats near the trash bins, it also struck me that I was pretty close to that gun, too.

Maybe a little *too* close.

CHAPTER 4

MISS GIDDINGS AND I STOOD IN THE SNOW, SILENT AND shivering, while more and more police officers and men from an ambulance joined us in the alley. Everybody around us was in motion, but the first officer who'd arrived had let us stand up, then told us not to move a muscle.

"The new Homicide Division don't like anything touched," he'd warned us. "And no chattering, either!"

I hoped that officer hadn't meant my *teeth*, because they were starting to chatter like crazy, while Miss Giddings seemed to be getting as numb and frozen as the corpse. She clutched her bloodstained fur coat with both hands, staring blankly, and the coroner had to ask her twice who the dead man was before she whispered, "Charles. Charles Bessemer."

Then, just when I thought I couldn't be a statue one second longer, a big dark sedan arrived, and I got my first glimpse of the Homicide Division. A man who had to be seven feet tall got out of the car and, as if he didn't even notice anyone standing there, parted the excited crowd that had gathered at the end of the alley. The automobiles' headlamps were behind him as he strode toward us, so I could see him only in silhouette, but the way his overcoat was flapping, he looked for all the world like the Grim Reaper. Like a guy who was gonna see *somebody* hang for what had just happened.

"I'm Detective James Culhane," he told me and Miss Giddings.

"Hey," I greeted him. "I'm Izzie. Nice to meetcha."

Apparently he didn't really care about making my acquaintance. He began pacing around the scene, studying everything—while I studied him. He wasn't as tall as I'd first thought, but he was at least a six-footer. And though I couldn't see much of his face, because his hat was pulled low, I could tell he wasn't smiling. He seemed to take forever examining the body, and I was relieved when he finally looked at me and Miss Giddings again —until he pointed to the weapon lying in the snow and asked, point-blank, "So, which one of you fired the gun?"

CHAPTER 5

I WASN'T BEING A SMART ALECK!" I PROTESTED AS A UNI-
formed officer hauled me into a bright, busy police
station. "I was just answering the detective!"

I still wasn't sure what I'd said to make Detective Culhane so angry. Well, except maybe the part about him
being crazy if he thought me or Miss Giddings could kill
anybody. I probably shouldn't have said—or shouted—
that.

"Will you please let me go?" I begged, trying to shake
free. "Please?"

"Just keep your mouth shut, kid," the policeman suggested. He continued to drag me along, so I wasn't sure
if I was officially under arrest. It seemed that way. "You'll
get plenty of time to talk when Detective Culhane questions you," he promised. "Save it for then!"

I thought the cops were also mad because I wouldn't
tell them how to find my mother. But if she had to leave
her job to help me, she might get fired, and then what?

Squirming, I looked over my shoulder to see that Detective Culhane was entering the station too, with a very frightened Miss Giddings in tow. I tried to give her a reassuring look, but she stared down at the floor, her shoulders hunched. The bloodstains on her coat had dried to brown, but they stood out even worse under the electric lights.

Ugh.

And just when it seemed like things were hectic enough, a bunch of men came out of nowhere, crowding around us and asking questions all at once.

"Who are they, Culhane?"

"What'd they do?"

"Look at the blood! The lady killed somebody, right? Another murderess!"

"Quiet down," Detective Culhane ordered them. "You'll get your story. Just be patient."

I understood then that the men were reporters—and they were following us deeper into the station, circling us, and jockeying for position while Detective Culhane ushered Miss Giddings into a chair near a messy desk. I was left standing, and the officer who'd escorted me kept one hand lightly on my elbow.

As I got my bearings, I looked closer at the reporters, only to discover that not all of them were men. There was one woman in the group. A lady I recognized from selling—and reading—the *Chicago Tribune*, which sometimes printed her picture.

Maude Collier, one of the only women in the entire nation who wrote about crime and other real news, just like men did. The woman I wanted to *be* someday.

Too bad I was finally meeting my heroine under such bad circumstances. And how the heck was I going to make a good first impression when Detective Culhane was insinuating that I was a cold-blooded killer? He leaned back against the desk, crossed his arms, and said to me and Miss Giddings, "Now, let's figure out how you two ended up in a dark alley with a corpse and a gun. Because I'm pretty confused."

He wasn't confused, though. He thought he knew the whole story—even if he was wrong.

Before Miss Giddings and I could defend ourselves, though, Maude Collier piped up, addressing Detective Culhane but managing to insult me.

"What are their names, Detective? And how is the *boy* involved?"

CHAPTER 6

HEY!" I CRIED, FINALLY SHAKING FREE OF THE OFFICER AND yanking off my cap so my brown curls sprang out in fifty different directions. "I'm a girl! My name's Isabel Feeney!"

More than once, I'd imagined what it would be like to meet Maude Collier in person. In my daydreams, I was a *Tribune* reporter too, and she stopped by my desk—I figured I'd have a desk—to congratulate me for scooping her on some big story.

I guess you're the star girl reporter now, Isabel Feeney, she'd tell me. *Nice work!*

In none of my fantasies did Miss Collier laugh at me, the way she and all the reporters did there in the police station. Even when she apologized, her mouth twitched, and there was an amused twinkle in her dark, intelligent eyes. "I'm very sorry, Miss Feeney. Please forgive me."

I was about to say it was okay—I *was* dressed in some of my father's old clothes—but before I could answer,

Detective Culhane growled, "Do you mind if I take over now, Maude?"

Jeez, what kind of bee was in his bonnet?

Miss Collier, who looked very professional with her black bobbed hair and straight skirt, didn't seem intimidated, though. She was still laughing. "Sure, Detective," she agreed. "Go ahead."

He gave her a long, dark look as he took off his hat, so I saw that he was actually fairly young. And his hair was almost black, like Miss Collier's. But his eyes were blue—and not twinkling. "Thanks," he finally grumbled. Then he turned to Miss Giddings. "So, tell me again where you were headed when a shot supposedly rang out of no-where—"

"It did come out of nowhere!" I interrupted. Detective Culhane clearly still didn't believe the story we'd told him in the alley. "That's how it happened!"

The detective, who was rolling up his shirtsleeves as if we were in for a long night, suddenly looked like *he* was going to commit a murder. He glared at me. "So you saw it, Miss Feeney? Saw the actual killing?"

My shoulders slumped. "No."

He didn't say anything else. He just turned slowly back to Miss Giddings, who was still in that awful stained coat. "Tell me the sequence of events again."

Miss Giddings's eyes were wide with fear, but she nodded. "As I said, Charles and I—"

Detective Culhane cut her short. "You mean Charles Bessemer—associate of Alphonse Capone?"

What?

I nearly fell over when he sprang *that* news on us. As everybody in Chicago—even kids—knew, Al Capone was a very dangerous man who'd made millions of dollars selling alcohol, which was illegal because of Prohibition. That's what the law had done. Made it unlawful to sell drinks like beer and wine anywhere in the United States. But people still bought liquor from crooks—who were called bootleggers. And the worst of the bootleggers was Al Capone, who had a bad habit of killing people who got in the way of his "business."

If Charles Bessemer worked for Al Capone, then Mr. Bessemer had been a criminal too.

But Miss Giddings would never spend time with someone like that . . .

The reporters in the room were scribbling furiously while I gave Miss Giddings an uncertain look. But she seemed as shocked as I was. Her face was pale, and she shook her head. "No . . . No! Charles was an automobile salesman," she protested. "He told me that!"

Detective Culhane didn't really do anything to show that he was skeptical, yet I could tell that he was. And when I looked at Miss Collier, she was rolling her eyes.

Why?

"We were going to get dinner," Miss Giddings continued, more calmly. "Taking a shortcut through the alley." Her face got even whiter. "And then I heard something—"

The detective's voice was sharp. "What? What did you hear?"

"A rustling sound," Miss Giddings said. "I looked toward it, thinking maybe it was a rat. Or something worse. I hadn't wanted to go through the alley. *Never* wanted to go that way!" She looked all around the room, as if she hoped someone would agree when she said, "This city . . . it's not safe."

Well, nobody could disagree with that, and some of the reporters nodded. Not Maude Collier, though. She kept her eyes trained on Miss Giddings, who added, "Then I heard a loud bang. And Charles . . ."

She couldn't seem to finish. Which was okay. We'd been through all of this about fifty times by that point.

But Detective Culhane loomed over poor Miss Giddings, his arms crossed, still challenging her. "How did the gun end up next to you?"

I glanced at Miss Collier and could tell that she mainly found the story entertaining, even when Miss Giddings buried her face in her hands, groaning, "I don't know . . . I don't know . . ."

"Is it yours?" Detective Culhane demanded. "The gun?"

Miss Giddings slowly straightened up. "No. It's not mine. I wouldn't have one. I have a boy—a son." She

glanced at me. "He's about Isabel's age. It's too dangerous to have a gun in the house. Boys get curious. Pick
things up . . ."

I'd forgotten about Robert. Was he worried? Should
his mom have been home by now?

I was so lost in thought that for a second I didn't
even realize that the room had gotten quiet. And when
I looked around, I discovered that everyone was staring
at me. Including Detective Culhane, who had apparently
asked me a question. A *new* question, which I'd sort of
hoped nobody would ever get around to asking.

"Well, Miss Feeney?" the imposing detective repeated,
staring hard at me. "What were Colette Giddings and
Charles Bessemer doing right before they turned down
that dark alley? What's the last thing you saw?"

Oh gosh, did I squirm. And I shot Miss Giddings a
very apologetic look before I confessed, with a quick,
nervous glance at the reporters who'd record every
word, "They . . . they seemed to be *fighting*."

CHAPTER 7

FIGHTING ABOUT WHAT?" DETECTIVE CULHANE ASKED ME. He leaned down, staring harder into my eyes. "Well?"

"I have no idea," I told him, getting exasperated. "I couldn't hear anything. It's windy out there, you know!"

Whatever I'd said made a couple of the adults in the room laugh.

Not Detective Culhane, though. He kept studying me. "So what makes you think . . ."

I gave Miss Giddings another apologetic look. I felt like I was betraying her. Then I told Detective Culhane, "I could see the expression on Miss Giddings's face. And the way Mr. Bessemer grabbed her arm. But it didn't look like a bad argument," I added. "I've had way worse fights with the kid next door—pounded him—but it doesn't mean I'd kill him!"

Wow, did everybody crack up then—except Detective Culhane. Well, Miss Collier didn't exactly laugh either. She was too busy scribbling in her notebook.

Was I going to be quoted in the newspaper?

Would Butchie McLaughlin slug *me* for letting the whole city know I beat him up sometimes—even if he did deserve it for calling us Feeneys "poor bums"? Just because my mother accepted his family's hand-me-down clothes didn't make *him* exactly rich!

Regardless, my answer seemed to satisfy Detective Culhane enough that he turned his attention back to Miss Giddings. "Well? Were you fighting?"

"Yes," she admitted. She looked down at her hands, fidgeting with a ring. A diamond ring I'd never noticed before, all the times she'd handed me money for papers. Was she *engaged?* "But it was only because I was late. Charles didn't like to be kept waiting."

Detective Culhane took a moment to think about that. His voice got quieter. "Did he get angry often?"

There was a long silence. Then Miss Giddings buried her face in her hands and her shoulders started to shake, so I realized she was crying.

Detective Culhane let her do that for a while; then he spoke to the reporters. "Go file your stories. We're done here. She's going over to the county jail for the night."

What?

"You can't arrest her!" I cried, jumping up. "You can't!"

But a police officer was already helping a very wobbly Miss Giddings stand up. Still, as she was led away, she managed to beg me, "Please, Isabel. Go tell my son what happened, and not to worry." She told me her address, which I hoped wouldn't fly right out of my head. And the next thing I knew, she was gone.

I would go find Robert that night. Of course, I'd do that.

But first I had something else to take care of.

I needed to make sure that Maude Collier didn't write a story that would lead a whole city—including potential jurors—to believe that Miss Giddings was guilty. Because I knew from reading all of Miss Collier's other articles that committing a cold-blooded murder in Chicago really could get a person *hanged*.

CHAPTER 8

MISS COLLIER!" I HOLLERED, RACING THROUGH THE POLICE station, right past an officer who was trying to offer me a ride home. "Miss Collier! Wait!"

She was reaching for a telephone, which hung on the wall, but she turned and gave me a funny look. "How do you know my name?"

"I . . . I . . ." I was out of breath, although I hadn't run that far. "I sell the *Tribune*," I finally wheezed out. "And I read your articles, all the time. You're famous."

She blinked about five times, as though I'd surprised her. I *was* probably one of the few kids who knew about her. I'd never sold a paper to anybody my age.

"Hey, Maude, you gonna call in your story? Because I'd like to use that telephone."

I looked around to find another reporter watching us, his arms crossed. But Miss Collier didn't seem worried about keeping him waiting. "Just relax, Tom," she said.

"Nobody reads the *Herald-Examiner*. You might as well go home to bed."

I knew that wasn't true. The *Herald-Examiner* was the *Tribune*'s big rival. But the reporter named Tom just grinned. I thought he kinda liked being teased. "Either talk to the kid or call in your story," he said. "I got an editor waiting."

Miss Collier still didn't take her hand off the telephone. "What do you want, Isabel?" she asked. "And it *is* Isabel, correct?"

If she used my name in an article, I wouldn't mind if she got it wrong, so I ignored the question. "I need to talk with you," I said, with a glance at the man from the *Herald-Examiner*. Lowering my voice, I explained, "I could tell you didn't believe Miss Giddings. But she's innocent. I know it."

I was pretty sure Miss Collier was going to tell me to get lost. But she didn't. She really looked me in the eyes, and something she saw there, I guess, made her pull her hand away from the telephone. Then she squeezed my shoulder. "Come on, Isabel. Let's talk."

Jeez, I hoped I could come up with something interesting, because all of a sudden I was worried. If I didn't have some big news to share, she might get awfully mad about giving up the chance to tell her story first.

Had I just made things worse for Miss Giddings by wasting a famous reporter's time?

It seemed possible. And yet I couldn't exactly say no when Miss Collier asked me, with a smile, the only *good* question I'd been asked that day.

"Would you like some hot cocoa?"

CHAPTER 9

THE FILLMORE DINER, ABOUT A BLOCK FROM THE POLICE station, smelled like heaven, and my mouth watered as Miss Collier greeted just about everybody in the place. And before we even sat down in a booth, somebody was setting a coffee mug on the table.

"Who's your friend, Maudie?" the waitress asked, jerking her head toward me. "Never saw you with a kid before."

"This is Isabel Feeney," Miss Collier said, taking off a cute cloche hat and shrugging out of her coat. Up close, she was even younger and prettier than I'd thought, with high cheekbones and a perfect smile that made me want to hide my crooked front tooth. "Isabel's had a long and difficult evening," Miss Collier added. "So I think some hot cocoa is in order." She looked across the table at me, arching a dark eyebrow. "And what will you eat, Isabel? You must be hungry."

I was near starving, but I had only a few coins in my

pocket. I was already worried that I'd said yes to the cocoa too fast, before learning if I'd have to pay, so—though I hadn't lied at the police station—I told a whopper in the diner. "I'm not hungry, thanks. I ate supper."

Of course, Miss Collier could tell I was lying. She didn't make a big show out of it, like I was a charity case, though. She just told the waitress, "Well, I am starving, Peg. I'll take two pieces of apple pie, please."

We both knew there'd be two forks, too, and although I was concerned about Miss Giddings, I couldn't help looking forward to some dessert. "Thanks, Miss Collier," I said. Then, just in case that extra pie *wasn't* for me, I added, "For talking to me, I mean."

"You're quite welcome, Isabel. And please, call me Maude."

My eyes got wide. "Really?"

"Sure, why not?"

"I've never called an adult by her first name," I admitted. "Thanks . . . Maude." It felt strange to say that, but I could probably get used to it. "And you can call me Izzie, if you want. That's what my friends do."

Maude's smile widened. "I'd like that, Izzie." Then she folded her arms on the table and leaned forward, growing more serious. "So why did you want to talk with me in particular? There were quite a few reporters at the station."

"But you're the best," I said honestly. "I read your stories all the time. You influence thousands of readers.

And sometimes you make people look awfully guilty. I don't want that to happen to Miss Giddings."

Maude's eyes clouded over. "Usually the people I cover *are* guilty, Isabel." Before I could protest, she suggested, "But tell me again . . . how did you really get mixed up in this whole mess?"

"I was just selling my papers—"

"Yes," Maude interrupted. "I was surprised when you mentioned that. Not too many girls sell newspapers."

I almost felt proud of my job for once, because a star reporter was looking at me with genuine interest. Like we shared a bond, both of us working in a business that was mainly for boys and men. Before I got too full of myself, I said, "Yeah, well, I really wish I could be like you. Writing news, not selling it."

Maude cocked her head. "Really?"

I nodded, hardly noticing that the waitress was slipping cocoa and pie under my nose. I got the feeling that Maude didn't think my dream was stupid. "Yeah," I confided. "I think your life must be really exciting." My cheeks got flushed a little, but I admitted, "And I like to write."

Maude wrapped her hands around her mug, warming them. "Tell me more."

"Well, I don't go to school anymore," I said through a mouthful of pie, because even an important conversation couldn't distract me forever. "I just make up stories sometimes, for fun. And I learn a lot by reading the *Tri-*

bune. Like how to write quotes and use punctuation . . . stuff like that."

"I'm impressed, Izzie," Maude said. "Very impressed."

I wasn't used to compliments, so I just shrugged. "Anyhow, I think you're about the luckiest person in the world. You get paid to write about all kinds of interesting things, and you're famous on top of that."

"I do enjoy my work," she agreed. "But it's not always easy being a woman in a man's sphere. Most newspapers don't even allow women to cover news. Women have to write about fashion, cooking, and things like weddings. Or they're assigned to do stunts—"

"Like Nellie Bly, going around the world in eighty days," I said. "I know all about her."

"And there are lots of other 'stunt girls,' who do dangerous things, then write about them," Maude continued. "But it's very rare for women to cover crime and other news, the way I do. Most news reporters are men because editors think women are too fragile to see blood."

"Like we did this evening." All of a sudden the pie didn't taste as good, and I got quieter. "It was pretty awful."

"Are you all right, Izzie?"

I nodded. "Yeah, I'll be okay." I knew we were getting off track, and I had other things to do that evening—like go see Robert—but I had to ask, "So how'd you do it?

How'd you get the job if newspapers don't usually hire lady reporters?"

Maude opened her mouth to answer. Then she no doubt remembered that if she wanted to *keep* writing about crime, she needed to get back to that telephone. "I'll tell you some other time. All right? I promise."

I was used to adult "promises"—which were never kept unless they involved me getting some kind of punishment—but I sort of believed her. Maybe because she was sliding her slice of pie across the table, without a word, so it joined my already empty plate. How could I not trust a woman who gave me *two* pieces of pie? Then, unfortunately, she took out her notebook and asked me a question I should've been prepared for—instead of daydreaming about being a big-shot journalist.

"So, what can you say to convince me that—unlike almost every other woman on Murderess's Row—this Miss Giddings is innocent?"

CHAPTER 10

IT FELT AS IF THE TEMPERATURE OUTSIDE HAD DROPPED TEN degrees while I'd been in the diner with Maude, and I ran down the street to keep warm, looking for the address Miss Giddings had given me.

Five thirty-one Throop Street.

I also ran because the neighborhood was dark and quiet, with most lucky families snug inside their little brick or wood-frame houses. I didn't want to be the second person killed in a lonely spot that night.

And as I hurried along, I tried to recall details from my talk with Maude.

Had I convinced her that Miss Giddings was innocent?

Looking back, it *seemed* like Maude had listened to me.

But had she ever come right out and said she believed me?

Maybe not, but we were *friends,* right?

It was too late to worry. I'd finally found the right address, and I bounded up onto the porch of a small brick bungalow. Raising my fist, I banged on the door, without even thinking about what I'd say to Robert. Which is probably why, when a pale, thin kid about my age opened the door just a crack and peeked out, the moonlight glinting off his eyeglasses, I blurted, "Let me in, Robert. We gotta help your mom."

CHAPTER 11

WHAT ARE YOU TALKING ABOUT?" THE PALE KID'S EYES were big with fear, and he kept the door almost shut, just peeping through the crack. "What happened to my mother?"

"She's okay," I promised. Then I realized that wasn't exactly true. "Kind of okay." I had been sweating inside my wool coat, and I started shivering now that I was standing still. "Can I come in, Robert?" I hesitated. "You *are* Robert, right?"

"Yes." He opened the door wider, and I took that to mean I could go inside.

Pushing past him, I stomped snow off my boots and looked around, thinking it was strange to be in Miss Giddings's house. The place wasn't fancy, but it was warm and tidy, unlike the house where I lived with my mother. Our place was cold and messy because Mom always seemed to have hard jobs, like cleaning the hospital, that left her too tired to fix things up at home. And I wasn't much help either, which was probably my own fault.

It was too bad my mother couldn't get an easier, better-paying clerk job, like Miss Giddings had.

Or could Mom do that?

Because she *was* pretty . . . and not *too* old . . .

"Who are you? And what happened to my mother?"

I'd been so busy coveting the clanking, hissing radiator, which was giving off glorious heat, and looking longingly at the furniture, which all matched, that I had almost forgotten Robert.

"I'm Isabel Feeney," I said, sticking out my hand. Robert seemed uncertain, but he shook it. His fingers were cold, in spite of the radiator. And when we pulled apart, he wobbled. This was the first time I noticed that he had a brace on one leg. A big metal thing that looked as if it had gobbled up everything from just above his left knee to his ankle. I tried to pretend I hadn't seen it. "Miss Giddings—I mean, your mother—is . . ." I started to say *in jail,* but that sounded too scary, so I said, "She's at the police station. The man she was going to eat dinner with tonight got shot." Robert's eyes got huge, but he didn't say anything, so I kept explaining. "I was there, selling newspapers, and she asked me to tell you."

Robert Giddings was pasty to begin with, but he was like a ghost by the time I got all that news out.

"Your mother didn't get hurt," I reassured him. "But Charles Bessemer is dead."

Oddly enough, Robert didn't react to that part—didn't so much as blink an eye—so I asked, "Did you know him? Mr. Bessemer?"

"Yes." He nodded slowly. "I know who he is." But I still couldn't tell if he was shocked or sad. Maybe he didn't feel anything. It seemed that way.

I peered more closely at Robert's face, trying to study his eyes behind those glasses.

Was there even a chance he was a little bit *happy* about Mr. Bessemer getting shot?

"Did your mom go out with Mr. Bessemer a lot?" I asked, partly because I was curious, but partly because the silence was getting uncomfortable.

Robert nodded. "Yes. A lot, lately."

He didn't seem like he was going to share more—or ask questions. Apparently, Robert Giddings wasn't exactly a chatterbox.

And what kind of kid didn't care about somebody getting shot dead?

Or *was* his reaction strange?

I looked around the snug little room again, just right for two people, and it struck me that I wouldn't know how to feel if my mother started going out on dates with a new man. I didn't think I'd want a different father. Okay, I *knew* I wouldn't want another father. Especially one who grabbed my mother the way I'd seen Mr. Bessemer grab Miss Giddings's arm.

Why had a person as nice as Miss Giddings spent

time with someone who treated her like that, even if she
hadn't known he was a mobster . . . ?

"When will my mother be home?" Robert finally
piped up, interrupting my thoughts. When he asked
about his mom, his voice sounded tight, as if he was
worried about her. Or maybe that brace was hurting
him because we were still standing. "Do you know?"

It was about time I told him the whole story—let
him know that his mother was *behind bars*—but before
I could say anything, there was a knock on the door. I
was pretty sure Miss Giddings would've just walked into
her own house, but I guess Robert wanted to see her so
badly, he didn't think about that, and he hobbled over to
twist the knob, muttering under his breath, "That must
be her."

But of course, it wasn't.

When Robert swung open the door, I saw none other
than Detective James Culhane.

And he looked about as happy to see me as I was to
see him.

Which wasn't very happy at all.

CHAPTER 12

"**Y**OU SEEM TO SHOW UP IN UNEXPECTED PLACES," DETECTIVE Culhane noted as he came into the house followed by another detective in a big overcoat. I remembered from the police station that the second man's name was Hastings. And although Detective Hastings might have been older, he was the assistant. At least it seemed to me that Detective Culhane was in charge. "I thought I had an officer drive you home," he added, making it sound as if I was doing something wrong. "Why are you here?"

Detective Culhane might have intimidated most people, but I *wasn't* doing anything wrong and had no reason to be scared. "I promised Miss Giddings I'd tell her son what happened," I said, giving him a level stare. "And I keep my promises."

Detective Culhane and I studied each other for a long moment. I could tell that he was a tiny bit impressed that I didn't cower before him like a whipped puppy. "Go on home now," he finally said. "Detective Hastings and I need to talk to Robert."

Poor Robert had been overlooked for a minute, but I had a feeling he liked it better that way. He didn't look too happy to be noticed. He also didn't seem to know what to say, and he turned to me, as if I had all the answers.

Ten minutes before, I hadn't known Robert Giddings from Adam, and we hadn't exactly become friends during our brief conversation, but in a split second we reached an understanding. Without even talking, we managed to agree that we needed to stick together. That his mother was in big trouble, that it was kids against adults, and that I *shouldn't* go home.

Turning back to Detective Culhane, I said, "Jeez! You're gonna send a kid out in the dark alone, so late? You're not gonna offer me another ride?"

A little muscle worked in his jaw. "You got here," he said evenly. "You can get home."

"Okay," I agreed, slumping my shoulders and dragging my feet toward the door. "I just hope *I* don't get shot!"

I had my hand on the doorknob for what seemed like forever—I really was going to have to turn it soon—when Detective Culhane said in a low, grudging growl, "Take a seat in the corner, Miss Feeney. And don't say another word."

I didn't even say thank you, for fear that he'd count

those as "other words" and boot me out into the snow. I just walked to where he was pointing and sat in a flower-patterned chair with a high back, near a radiator that was starting to give off too much heat, given that I still wore my father's old wool cap. When I pulled it off, my mess of sweaty brown hair sprang out even wilder than before, so I kind of wished I'd just kept the hat on.

The heavyset, bald Detective Hastings stifled a laugh, pretending to cough into his hand, while Detective Culhane scowled harder at me, as if even my hair angered him. Then he turned to Robert, who was still standing by the door, and even though the room was pretty dark, lit by one electric lamp, I saw him glance at Robert's leg. To my surprise, the tough, stern policeman's expression softened just a tiny bit. He didn't sound quite as gruff, either, when he urged, "Have a seat, Robert."

I wasn't sure if Robert's leg actually hurt — he'd probably had polio, and I heard you couldn't feel anything if it got your legs or arms — but it was painful for *me* to watch him hobble across the room, his head hanging down. We all studied him in silence, so the squeak that his brace made with every step sounded like a scream. I breathed a sigh of relief when he finally sank down onto a wooden rocking chair, close to the lamp.

Detective Hastings started to sit too, but one sharp look from Detective Culhane sent him springing back to his feet. "Sorry, sir," he mumbled, his face red.

Yup. Detective Culhane was definitely in charge.

He returned his attention to Robert, and any compassion he'd felt for a kid with a bad leg was either gone or hidden. He spoke bluntly. "Your mother was at the scene of a shooting this evening. A man named Charles Bessemer is dead."

Robert nodded. "Yes." He pointed at me. "She told me."

Well, thanks so much for remembering my name.

"I'm Isabel," I reminded Robert—forgetting that I wasn't supposed to speak. Detective Culhane gave me the evil eye. "Sorry," I muttered, sounding like Detective Hastings, who I swore shot me a sympathetic look from where he stood near the fireplace. "I'll stay quiet now," I promised—making the mistake of talking *again*.

Detective Culhane didn't respond. He resumed speaking with Robert. "What do you know about Mr. Bessemer?"

Robert adjusted his spectacles and raised big, uncertain eyes to Detective Culhane. "I don't know . . . I think he sells . . . sold . . . automobiles. Packards. He drove a new Packard. The neighbors would always come out and admire it when it was parked here."

"Yes, I've heard that story," Detective Culhane muttered. "Anything else?"

"Mr. Bessemer has . . . had . . . a daughter, named Flora," Robert noted. "I only met her once, but she was going to be my sister, I guess."

So Miss Giddings *had* been engaged. And poor Robert had been about to get not just a new father but a sibling, too. Living next to Butchie McLaughlin, who had seven of those, I could *really* understand why Robert hadn't seemed overly upset about Mr. Bessemer getting shot. Brothers and sisters looked like nothing but trouble to me. And from the sour expression on Robert's face when he said Flora's name, I had a feeling she wasn't exactly charming.

Detective Culhane didn't seem interested in Mr. Bessemer's offspring, though. "Did your mother and Mr. Bessemer ever fight?" he asked. "Did you ever see them argue? Or see Mr. Bessemer push or hit your mother?"

Robert must've been a smart kid. I could tell that he was figuring out the stuff I hadn't told him. I knew he was grasping that his mother wasn't there—and the police were—because she hadn't just *seen* a shooting. She was a suspect. A woman who'd maybe been pushed around one too many times.

Robert stayed very quiet. But the way he swallowed, really hard, said way too much.

I was confused.

Seriously . . . why had Miss Giddings wasted her time with a man who'd been mean to her?

I was trying to figure that out when Detective Culhane asked another question that I thought would finally begin to clear everything up.

"Does your mother own a gun, Robert?"

It was adults against kids in that room, and Robert looked at me again for some sort of silent advice.

Fortunately, I had heard Miss Giddings tell the police that she would never, ever own a gun, so I smiled and nodded at him, as if to say, *Just tell the truth!*

Which, apparently, is what Robert did. Only his truth was different from Miss Giddings's.

As I watched with a sick feeling in my stomach, Robert raised his nervous green eyes to meet Detective Culhane's shrewd blue ones and said, weakly, "Yes. Yes, she does."

CHAPTER 13

'D BEEN TOLD TO SIT IN MY CHAIR WHILE ROBERT SHOWED the detectives where his mother supposedly kept the gun she'd sworn she didn't have, but I couldn't stay still. I *had* to know what was happening upstairs in Miss Giddings's bedroom.

My own mother always said curiosity was going to get me killed, which didn't stop me from creeping over to the staircase and crawling, on all fours, up to the top.

What if Robert needed me?

Plus I just had to know why Miss Giddings had lied. She *must* have had a good reason.

". . . in this drawer?" Detective Culhane was asking when I got within earshot.

I peeked down the hall and saw light coming from an open doorway.

"Yes," Robert confirmed as I crawled closer. "In there."

By hugging the wall and staying in the shadows, I was

able to find a safe spot where I could see most of what was happening. Detective Hastings stood next to the bed, yawning and eyeing the soft-looking quilt as if he wanted to lie down, while Detective Culhane reached out to open the top drawer of Miss Giddings's bureau.

If intruding on a lady's most private belongings bothered him, it didn't show. In fact, Robert and I were the only ones who blushed when Detective Culhane pulled out a bunch of "unmentionables" in a big clump in his hand.

Well, Detective Hastings looked uncomfortable too. He made a "harrumph" sound into his fist and looked down at the floor.

Detective Culhane didn't even seem to notice that he was holding lacy things, the straps dangling down from his fingers. He gave Robert a sharp glance. "You're certain this is where she kept the gun?"

Robert nodded. "Yes, sir. She told me never to touch it." He got redder. "She joked that she knew I'd never go in *that* drawer."

In spite of the bad circumstances, I thought that was pretty funny, and I almost laughed. I also wondered how a bubbly person like Miss Giddings had gotten such a drab kid like Robert, who didn't seem to find that logic even slightly amusing.

Detective Culhane wasn't laughing either. He turned to poor Hastings, who was stifling yet another yawn. "The gun's not here now," Detective Culhane told his assistant. "There's nothing in here but undergarments." While Robert and Hastings squirmed again, he crammed the lacy stuff back into the drawer. "Did you ever see your mother move the gun?" he asked Robert. "Did she ever take it with her?"

Robert shook his head. "No." He paused, then added uncertainly, "I don't think so."

Boy, did old Hastings—who I was starting to like, even if he hardly said a word—look disappointed when Detective Culhane turned and ordered him, "Telephone the station and get some uniformed officers over here. I want this house searched thoroughly for that gun, in case she *did* move it." It was clear that he believed the weapon had already been found, though—in an alley, next to Charles Bessemer's body. "You take over the search, Hastings," he added grimly. "Because I need to talk to Miss Giddings again."

"Yeah, sure," Detective Hastings agreed, with one last, longing glance at the bed. Then he looked at Robert. "Do you have someplace to stay tonight, son?" he asked kindly. "This may take a while, and you'll need some sleep."

They started to confer quietly while I began to backtrack down the hallway. Any second now, Detective Culhane, who was deep in thought, rubbing his jaw and staring into the drawer of undergarments, would come downstairs, expecting to find me in a chair, probably dozing off.

Then again, maybe he'd known I'd been crouching outside the room the whole time. Without even glancing in my direction, he said, "Stand up, Miss Feeney. I'm not going to watch you crawl *down* a flight of stairs like an awkward cat."

There was no use trying to pretend I wasn't hiding, so I got to my feet.

And before I could apologize — again — Detective Culhane came over to the door and clapped one powerful hand on my shoulder, steering me toward the staircase. "I'll take you home now."

It was a nice offer, but I couldn't help feeling that I'd just been arrested for the second time that night.

I was also probably pressing my luck when I twisted around to look up at Detective Culhane's grave countenance and asked, "Can I at least talk to Robert before we go?"

CHAPTER 14

"HEY, DO YOU REALLY HAVE A PLACE TO SLEEP TONIGHT?"
I asked Robert after pulling him into the kitchen,
where we could talk in private. I could hardly believe
Detective Culhane had given us time alone, but he'd
grunted "one minute" and left to wait in his automobile.
"You could come to my house," I offered, even though
my mother wouldn't be happy with me bringing home
the son of a lady who'd be all over the papers as a murder suspect the next day.

*What will Maude write? Something good, of course, after
our talk . . .*

I shook off my worry and asked the silent Robert
again, "You need a place to stay?"

"No, thanks," he said. "I have an aunt who lives a few
blocks away. She might help me out, at least for tonight."

I couldn't help thinking, *Nice aunt!* Because what kind
of relative "might" help a kid for one stinkin' night?

"Detective Hastings is going to take me there and explain what happened," Robert added.

"Yeah, he seems all right," I noted, with a glance at the door in case the *other* detective hadn't really gone outside. "Unlike you-know-who!"

Robert looked to the door too. "Yes. Detective Culhane's intimidating."

"Nice word." I peeked at Robert's brace. "You read a lot, huh?"

That probably wasn't the right thing to say, but Robert didn't seem to mind. "I have a lot of time, and I like books."

"I read too," I admitted. "And write. Sometimes." Then I blurted a secret I'd told only one other person, just recently in a coffee shop. "I'm going to be a reporter someday."

Robert didn't act like that was strange. Maybe he had secret dreams too. Had plans to do things that, because of his leg, people would say he couldn't do, just like most people thought a girl couldn't be a real reporter. Regardless, he and I looked at each other—really sized each other up—for a long time. "My mother's in big trouble, isn't she?" he finally ventured, quietly.

I could've lied to make him feel better, but he deserved the truth. "Yeah," I said. "But I'll help you both."

"What can *you* do?" Robert asked. He wasn't being rude. He honestly wanted to know.

"I'm not sure." Then I thought of Maude Collier. "But

I know somebody who can at least give me information. Someone who will talk to your mom if they keep her in jail."

Robert looked queasy. "Do you think that might really happen?"

"I don't know," I said. But I read the newspapers—followed the cases Maude covered—and I knew that some accused criminals spent weeks or even months in jail, waiting for their trials. Robert didn't need to worry about that yet, though, so I asked another question that was bothering me. "Are you *sure* your mom had a gun?"

Because that would make her a liar. At least about that.

"I haven't seen it for a long time," Robert said, telling me something he should have told Detective Culhane. But who could think straight when he glared at you? "Maybe she got rid of it," he added. "She was anxious about having it in the house."

I thought *anxious* was a good word too.

"The gun was my father's," Robert continued with a glance down at his bad leg. "Or used to be . . ."

I wanted to hear what had happened to his dad, but before I could ask, Detective Hastings poked his head into the kitchen. "You better get going, kid," he told me. "You don't want to keep Detective Culhane waiting." He rolled his eyes. "Believe me, I know."

I was liking Hastings more and more.

"I'm coming," I said. Then I squeezed Robert's arm. "I'll be back, okay?"

The offer wasn't much, but Robert jumped on it. "Promise?"

I spit in my palm and held it out. "Promise."

Robert gave my hand a disgusted look right before we shook for a second time. I felt good about befriending a boy who probably didn't have a lot of pals—until it hit me that I didn't have a lot of friends either. I mean, sure, I knew people I sold papers to, like Miss Giddings and some other regular customers. But most of the time, I was just alone.

"I'll see you tomorrow, okay?" I said, only to realize that I didn't know where he'd be. "At your aunt's house—or here?"

Robert looked down at his bum leg again. "Probably here."

I hoped he was wrong, and that his aunt would watch out for him, but I said, "Okay. I'll come here. Probably kinda late, after my mom goes to work."

"Miss Feeney . . ." Detective Hastings prompted me, but in a nice way. "Get a move on!"

"Okay, okay." I headed for the front door, ran out into the cold night, and climbed into the front seat of a warm, rumbling sedan. Detective James Culhane was waiting for me, drumming his fingers on the steering wheel. At first I was just happy that the automobile had a heater, because I'd never been in one that fancy before. But when my chauffeur turned to look at me—heater or no heater—I got chilly inside to see his most profoundly

unhappy expression so far. And that was saying something.

Reaching blindly for the door handle, I started to say
that I'd just as soon walk, even if I got shot or something.

But before I could find a way out, Detective Culhane
put the automobile in gear, and there was nothing I
could do but brace myself for what was bound to be a
very bad conversation.

And yet that whole ride . . . it turned out different
than I ever could've expected.

CHAPTER 15

WHILE I'D ANTICIPATED A LECTURE ON THE DANGERS OF getting mixed up in a murder investigation, it took me only about two blocks to realize that Detective Culhane could *really* make me squirm just by being quiet.

He could do silent even better than Robert Giddings.

Unfortunately, I could never shut up. "This is a very nice car," I said, reaching for a knob. In a split second, Detective Culhane's right hand snatched my fingers, stopping me.

"Don't touch anything," he warned. Then he let go of me. "Please."

"Jeez, sorry!" I crossed my arms. "I wasn't going to break anything."

We got quiet again—until he made what I thought was a wrong turn. "You sure you know where you're going?" I asked, trying to be helpful.

"Yes." That little muscle in his jaw twitched again. "I think I know this city."

I shifted to get a better look at him. "You grow up here?"

He gave me a quick look. "Yes." That was all. Apparently, he didn't like answering questions. Only asking them. "You're out awfully late, alone," he noted, returning his attention to the street. "Where are your parents? Your family? Why aren't they worried?"

"My mother cleans at night," I told him. "She thinks I'm home." I picked a stray thread off the hat on my lap. "And my dad died in the war."

Detective Culhane frowned at me—but not in his usual angry way. "Sorry."

He sounded sincere, and when he faced forward again, I studied his profile in the dark. He was probably about the age my father would've been if he'd survived the Great War, and forgetting for a moment that Detective Culhane wasn't eager to talk about himself, I asked, "Were you in the war?"

As soon as the words were out, I realized he probably wouldn't answer. So I was surprised when he nodded. "Yes. Infantry. France."

That was all he said, and it was clear he thought even that was too much.

I wanted to ask more because infantry . . . they were the soldiers like my dad, who'd actually done the fighting, from long lines of deep trenches dug into the earth. I'd overheard my mother say that infantry saw terrible things in those muddy burrows, and I would've liked to hear what it had really been like for my father.

Maybe Detective Culhane had even met my dad.

All of a sudden I got sick to my stomach because, although it was unlikely—thousands of soldiers had fought in France—it struck me that Detective Culhane might've served with my dad and even *seen him die*. Might know the whole story, and if my father had suffered, like from poison gas the Germans had used, or if he'd gone quickly, like from a bullet. Or if it had been *really* horrible, from a bayonet . . .

I was glad when Detective Culhane changed the subject, asking in a grudgingly kinder voice, "Are you hungry, Isabel?"

Of course I was hungry. I'd covered quite a few miles since eating those two slices of pie. But I was also tired and wanted to go home. Plus I wasn't sure how long Detective Culhane would stay softened up, so I said, "Not really."

The sedan was dark inside, but I could tell he didn't believe me.

"Really," I reassured him. "I ate some pie with Maude Collier."

He gave me a sharp glance. "What?"

"I had to convince her not to make Miss Giddings look

guilty," I explained. "Because I read her stories, and she's not very nice to criminals." I needed to fix that. "I mean, to people she *thinks* are criminals. Which Miss Giddings is *not*."

"Oh, Isabel . . ." We'd reached my rundown old house —somehow he had found the way—and he stopped the car, turned off the motor, then sighed and rubbed his forehead with his fingers. Apparently I'd said something wrong again. He shifted to face me, and the lecture finally started. "You shouldn't be speaking with reporters, however 'pretty' and 'charming' they may seem—"

Whoa! Hold on there!

"Are you sweet on her?" I blurted. Because, really— "pretty" and "charming"?

"No!" he said too quickly, and I thought, *Gosh, he really is!*

I fought the urge to grin while he composed himself. "My point is, you shouldn't be insinuating yourself into a murder investigation," he advised me. "This is not a game, Miss Feeney."

"I know it's not," I told him. "Miss Giddings could *hang!*"

Detective Culhane got quiet again. Then he said, very seriously, "You're correct, Isabel. She could be executed. Perhaps *should* be executed. But it's unlikely. Women almost never hang in Cook County, Illinois."

"But she could. You just said it."

Detective Culhane didn't argue. Instead, he surprised

me by asking, "What do you really know about Miss Giddings?"

I took a moment to consider that. "I know that she's nice . . . and a good person," I finally ventured. My answer sounded weak, even to me. "She always gives me a tip when she buys a paper. And she asks about me . . . *really* asks, not like most people do."

That all sounded flimsy too, and we both knew it.

"I've seen a lot of cases like this," Detective Culhane informed me. "And usually, the pattern is the same. A man and a woman fight—maybe often. Someone has a gun. Things end badly."

"It's not like that with Miss Giddings," I insisted. "Robert thinks she might've gotten rid of the gun ages ago. And you said Charles Bessemer was a gangster. Maybe he got shot because of that!"

Detective Culhane didn't seem interested in my ideas. "Stay out of this, young lady," he ordered me, as though I were Hastings. Then he nodded toward my house, dismissing me. "Good night."

"Good night," I grumbled. I pulled the handle and opened the heavy door. "See ya."

"No," I heard him say. "I won't see you—"

I slammed the door before he could make me promise to keep my nose out of Miss Giddings's troubles, because I couldn't do that. Especially after I went to sell my papers the next day, tired from being up too late, tossing and turning in bed, my nightmares filled with murder and polio and men fighting in trenches. I was pretty bleary-eyed, but I could still read the headline for a story on the front page of the *Tribune*. An article written by my *friend* Maude Collier.

Oh. No.

CHAPTER 16

"PRETTIEST" SLAYER NABBED FOR ALLEY MURDER

Single Bullet Kills Cruel Suitor

by Maude Collier

Cook County Jail's infamous "Murderess's Row" has a new and comely resident.

Police last night arrested pretty department store clerk Colette Giddings after she was discovered kneeling next to the bleeding body of her boyfriend, smalltime gangster Charles "the Bull" Bessemer.

The coroner attributed Bessemer's death to a single bullet, fired at close range into his temple.

Miss Giddings, between bewildered blinks of innocent brown eyes, was quick to distance herself from a gun found within convenient reach of her hand, which sported an impressive diamond, courtesy of Bessemer.

The gun, meanwhile, sported Giddings's fingerprints.

"I don't own a gun," she insisted during questioning. "Guns are too dangerous. I only touched it because it was lying there, and I panicked!"

Pulling a bloodstained fur—also a gift from Bessemer—more closely around herself, she similarly denied knowledge of "the Bull's" connection to the head of Chicago's infamous mob aristocracy, one Alphonse Capone.

"I just thought Charles sold automobiles," the guileless clerk claimed with a confused pout. "I didn't know he dealt in alcohol!"

Alcohol . . . autos . . . an easy mistake!

Questioned by Detective James Culhane, *Tribune* newsgirl Isabel Feeney, first on the scene after the killing, said she'd seen the couple exchange angry words moments before the shot rang out in a dark, secluded alley off Wabash Avenue.

Reporters and detectives laughed as Miss Feeney also pointed out that she frequently "pounded" a neighbor boy—but "it doesn't mean I'd kill him!"

Despite the girl's persuasive argument on behalf of Miss Giddings, Detective Culhane nevertheless ordered the city's latest man-killer to spend some restorative time in the Cook County Jail, where she awaits the results of a coroner's jury . . .

That was all I bothered to read. With steam coming out of my ears into the icy February air, I tore the story out of the paper and tossed the rest to the ground. But as I crumpled the article to jam it into my pocket, I noticed some photos, one of which showed Charles Bessemer with a snooty-looking girl in ribbons and bows, who must've been his daughter, Flora. And even though I felt sorry for her, losing her dad too, I couldn't help thinking, *No wonder Robert didn't look too happy about getting a sister!*

I uncrumpled the paper and looked closer.

But why did Flora seem familiar to me?

Kneeling down, I grabbed the *Trib* again and turned a few pages until I found her where she always was—in an advertisement in the section meant for ladies, with stories about cooking and sewing. Flora was standing next to a pretty woman in an apron, both of them smiling in a sticky-sweet way. Flora held up a slice of bread, next to the quote, "Mommy only buys our family Bakery Pride Bread. It keeps me healthy and her young!"

Gosh . . . Flora Bessemer was the Bakery Pride girl! *She must be rich.*

Then, though I knew I might lose my job and be even poorer if anybody told on me for abandoning my corner, I left the whole stack of papers next to a lamppost and stalked off, headed for the massive new Tribune Tower building on Michigan Avenue to give Miss Maude Collier a piece of my mind about how she'd portrayed Miss Giddings.

And this time, I wouldn't be bought with a few slices of pie.

CHAPTER 17

I WAS FULL OF OUTRAGE—UNTIL I STOOD ACROSS BUSTLING Michigan Avenue, gawking at the soaring, spiky, brand-spanking-new Tribune Tower, which had to be the biggest and most beautiful building in the world. I knew from reading the paper that there'd been an international competition to design it, and the architect who'd won had modeled it after a famous cathedral in France.

But I'd never seen a church that touched the sky the way the Tower did. God himself might've tripped on the thing if he was walking around up in the clouds.

And I knew I'd find stones and bricks inside from the world's most famous structures, like the Great Wall of China and the ancient Italian Colosseum. The *Trib*'s stories about construction had always mentioned those artifacts and bragged about how the Tower would be just as well-known as those foreign sites.

I'm standing in front of history—and a place where history is made.

In spite of how angry I was, I couldn't help wishing, more than ever, that I could work in such an important building and make *my* mark on the city and the planet. Yet at the same time, that dream never seemed more out of reach.

Dodging autos and delivery carts, I hurried across Michigan Avenue in my heavy boots, wondering how I, Isabel Feeney, who didn't even go to school, could think about being a news reporter in a skyscraper with an arched entrance that was at least twenty feet high.

Talk about dreaming too big!

But of course I wasn't there to apply for a job that day. I was there to give Maude Collier a piece of my mind.

Taking a deep breath, I joined the flow of people going in and out of that doorway.

It wasn't until I was inside the grandest room I'd ever seen that I realized I had no idea how I'd find one woman in a building where it seemed like thousands of people were scurrying around, all of them seeming to know where they were headed.

Gathering up all my courage, I grabbed the sleeve of the closest person, tugging hard to get noticed.

Needless to say, *that* went wrong.

CHAPTER 18

WHADDYA WANT, KID?" A GRUFF MAN DEMANDED, PULLING the sleeve of his overcoat free of me. He scowled worse than Detective Culhane, and wasn't half as handsome, so it came off even scarier, if that was possible. "Whaddaya doin' here?"

"Are you a reporter?" I asked. "I'm looking for—"

He cut me off. "I'm an adman. Don't know the reporters."

Gosh, was the place *that* big? And what was an adman?

"Can you at least tell me where the reporters work?" I inquired, grabbing his sleeve again because he was starting to walk away, into the crowd of people who kept sidestepping us. "Please?"

"We're awfully busy here," he said, prying at my fingers. "Let go!"

"Walter!"

A woman's voice interrupted, and I felt a gentle hand

on my shoulder. Turning, I saw that a very pretty young lady in a modern short skirt, a ruffled blouse, and eyeglasses was smiling at the man named Walter. "What are you doing to this poor child?" she asked, hugging a big stack of papers to her chest. "Huh?"

Walter blushed and got less gruff. "He's just lost or somethin' . . ."

"Hey!" I pulled off my cap, letting my hair spring free.

The lady was also correcting the mistake. "She's a girl, Walter!"

Walter's face got even redder, but he didn't apologize.

"Go on," the nice woman told him with a nod. "I'll help her. You run along."

"Fine." Walter shuffled off, grumbling about "kids" and "dames," while the kind lady bent down, smiling again. "How can I help you, sweetie?"

"I'm looking for Maude Collier," I said. "I need to give her a piece of my mind."

The young woman reared back. Her eyes twinkled with amusement. "Is that so?"

She might've found the whole thing funny, but I was dead serious. "Yeah. You know where I can find her—"

"Miss Dalton," she said. "My name is Lizzie Dalton. And you are . . ."

"Isabel Feeney. *Tribune* newsgirl."

I added that last part so Miss Dalton might think I belonged in the Tribune Tower. And the announcement did make her smile wider. "Well, Isabel Feeney, Maude

Collier is a very busy, and famous, woman. She's one of the paper's top reporters, you know!"

"I think she'll see me," I predicted. "We're kind of . . . friends."

Until I yell at her.

"Oh!" Miss Dalton's eyebrows shot up with surprise. "Well then, Isabel, come along with me." Taking my shoulder again, she steered me toward a row of big gold doors. I knew they were elevators, even though I'd never been in one. "I suppose I can at least take you to the city room."

I glanced up, confused. "City room?"

"That's where Miss Collier and the other news reporters work."

"Oh." I acted as if I already knew that—and allowed myself to be maneuvered into a closet operated by a man in a gold-buttoned suit, looking like he was in the army. All at once, as Miss Dalton and a few other people followed me, cramming into the box, I wondered just how high we were going and how strong the ropes or wires that would pull us were. I wasn't too keen on heights, or tumbling out of the sky, for that matter. "Ummm . . ."

But before I could ask if there was a staircase we could use, everybody, including Miss Dalton, started calling out numbers to the uniformed man, and the next thing I knew, the floor moved. It took me all of two seconds to get queasy, and I rested my hand on my stomach, thinking that Colonel McCormick, who ran the whole paper, probably wouldn't like me messing up his elevator. How could Miss Dalton be so nonchalant?

"You a reporter too?" I asked, suddenly wondering if being a female journalist wasn't so special after all. There were a lot of women in that building.

"No," she said quietly, so I got that an elevator was one of those places where you should whisper. Like a church. "I take orders for advertisements — over the telephone," she explained proudly. "Men like Walter go out to businesses and sell advertising, while girls like me answer telephones when people call in to place a classified."

I knew what she meant. The main pages of the newspaper featured big, picture-filled advertisements for department stores like Marshall Field's, where Miss Giddings worked. Then there was a separate part of the paper for regular people who wanted to sell things, such as a rug they didn't want anymore. Those "classified" advertisements were small and not as important.

I looked up at Miss Dalton, puzzled. "How come men get to go out all over the city and women get stuck answering telephones?"

She frowned. "It's just . . . the way it's done," she said as the elevator stopped, the doors opened, and two men exited. Apparently we hadn't arrived yet, though, because Miss Dalton didn't move. "It's not respectable — or safe — for women to run around the city knocking on doors," she added. "Men are just better suited for that kind of work."

She could probably tell that I wasn't certain about that. It seemed to me that women were getting a bad deal. Maude Collier, at least, "ran around" the city at all hours. But I didn't want to hurt Miss Dalton's feelings, so I nodded. "Sure."

Just then the elevator stopped again, and the operator opened the door. "This is your floor, Isabel," Miss Dalton told me. "Just go on in and ask for Miss Collier. Everybody knows her." Right before the door closed, she called, "And keep your ears covered when you walk through, Isabel! It's not couth in there!"

I barely heard Miss Dalton, or felt the push of her hand on my back, which sent me into a space that was even more amazing than the Tribune Tower's deluxe grand entrance. Not because this place was fancy. It was actually a mess.

In my opinion, though, the "city room" looked and smelled and sounded . . . *incredible.*

CHAPTER 19

THE *TRIBUNE'*S FIRST FLOOR HAD BEEN BUSY, BUT THE CITY room was *chaos,* a tornado of motion and noise, filled with important people doing the important work of getting and telling the stories about the characters who made Chicago such a dangerous, thrilling, funny, scary place to live. The diamond-studded gangsters and cold-hearted gun girls and greedy speakeasy operators and ruthless rumrunners . . .

I really want to work here!

My heart pounding, I stood for a moment, just taking it all in. The large room was filled with men shouting into telephones, smoking cigars and cigarettes, saying words that would've made my mother wash out my mouth with soap, and jumping out of their chairs to hurry . . . who knew where?

Men . . . They really are almost all men . . .

And then I found her. The woman I'd come to see. She stood surrounded by male reporters, holding court, and in spite of her skirt, her sleek bobbed hair, and her lipstick, she was laughing with them like one of the boys.

Well, she wouldn't be laughing long.

When I saw Maude Collier, my anger came rushing back, and I strode right up to her, pushing through that circle of men. Jabbing my finger at her, I snapped, "You have a lot of nerve!"

CHAPTER 20

ISABEL, WHAT ARE YOU DOING HERE?" MAUDE ASKED WHILE the men around her all guffawed. Apparently, my being angry was amusing to them. I never quite knew why adults found me so funny. At least Maude wasn't laughing. "Quiet, boys," she told them with a warning look. She made a shooing motion with her hand. "Go on, now."

That city room might've been boys' territory, but they all listened to Maude and drifted off, although they were still grinning and saying things like "Good luck with that one, Maudie!"

She ignored them and turned to me with concern in her dark eyes. "Is everything all right, Isabel? What's going on?"

I didn't exactly answer her questions, because she was the one who needed to explain herself. "How could you make Miss Giddings look so terrible in the paper?" I demanded, pretty loudly. "We had an agreement!"

"No, Isabel," Maude said softly. She knitted her brows, as if she were confused, and guided me into a chair next to her desk. Then she sat down too. Her chair had wheels, which made it better than mine. And her desk was a mess, filled with papers, so you could hardly find the telephone. It all looked like heaven to me. "I never promised you that I'd cast your Miss Giddings in *any* sort of light."

I supposed that was technically true. But we'd had hot cocoa, and pie, and such a nice time, and I *thought* she'd listened to me and taken me seriously . . .

"My job is to write stories as I see them," Maude continued. "And everything I wrote was true."

"Even about Miss Giddings's fingerprints being on the gun?" I challenged her. "Because I didn't hear anything about that at the police station!"

"I didn't make that up," Maude assured me. "That report came in late, after you left."

"But—"

"I *promise* you, Isabel," she interrupted. "My story was accurate."

I thought back to the article, and how Maude had included stuff about Miss Giddings's bloodstained coat, and the diamond Charles Bessemer had given her, and the way she'd acted innocent about the gun, and I had to admit that it had all been true. But I'd seen things another way.

"When I have your job, I'll do it different," I muttered. "I'll be *fair* to people!"

Maude didn't respond for a moment. "Perhaps you will be a different kind of reporter, Isabel," she finally said, seriously. "Perhaps this business will be different for all women by the time you are a journalist. And maybe this city will be different, too."

She seemed almost sad, and I wasn't sure why. It softened me toward her just a little. But I still told her, "It wasn't nice of you to make fun of me, either." I'd started twisting my cap in my hands, and when I looked up, Maude was offering me candy from a bowl she'd dug out from under those papers. I was angry, but I didn't get sweets very often, and I took some. Maybe five pieces. Or six. I wouldn't let her bribe me again, though, and I asked, "How could you do that to me?"

Maude frowned. "But Isabel . . . that anecdote about your neighbor was charming! I didn't mean to embarrass you!"

Yeah, right. Cramming the butterscotches into my coat—and taking a few more, since the bowl was still within reach—I stood up, trying to act indignant. "You have a lot of power in this city, Maude." Using her first name still felt a little strange, but I forged ahead. "People are going to read that article and think Miss Giddings killed Charles Bessemer."

"The evidence points that way—"

What "evidence" was there, really? Besides a gun, some blood, fingerprints, a lie on Miss Giddings's part . . . Okay, maybe there was some evidence.

"—and Detective Culhane seems convinced," Maude continued, smiling in a funny way, given that we were talking about murder. "He's an excellent judge of these things, and his first instincts are usually correct."

Good grief. Was *she* sweet on *him?*

It sure seemed possible. Her cheeks were a little flushed when she concluded, "My own experience leads me to agree with James."

Did she just call old stone face "James"?

Yes, she did!

I wasn't concerned about a potential romance between a detective and a reporter right then, though. I was scared for an innocent department store clerk and her son.

"If Miss Giddings ends up hanging," I told Maude, "and poor, crippled Robert is left alone—that will be on *your* conscience."

Maude didn't seem worried. Just intrigued. The reporter part of her was gleaming in her eyes again. "Who is Robert?"

As usual, I'd said too much. "Nobody."

Maude's eyes softened. She'd no doubt figure out who Robert was later. It wouldn't be that hard. "Come have lunch with me, Isabel," she offered. "I would like to apologize for embarrassing you in the paper, although that was never my intent."

My stomach was growling, but I had my pride too. I

wouldn't take more than candy, that day. "No, thanks," I said, standing up. "I have someplace to go."

Maude rose too. "Where, Isabel?"

I wasn't sure if she was asking as a friend—or a journalist.

Either way, given my destination, I didn't plan to tell *her*.

CHAPTER 21

I WASN'T SURE WHAT I EXPECTED TO FIND IN THE ALLEY WHERE Charles Bessemer got shot. I mean, the police had looked over every single inch. I knew that because I'd had to stand in the freezing cold while they did it. But they had searched at night, and I was there in broad daylight.

And boy, did things look different.

Well, kind of different.

There was still some blood on the snow, and it seemed to me that somebody should've cleaned it up. And there were a lot of footprints around where the body had been, most of them coming from the same direction, where the police had all parked their cars.

But . . .

I looked farther down the alley, which obviously didn't get used a lot. There were hardly any tire marks or footprints beyond the big mess made by the police.

Miss Giddings said she heard a noise, like a rat, then a gunshot.

And the coroner said Mr. Bessemer was shot at close range . . .

Stepping around the blood, I ignored the footprints in the middle of the alley and headed for a bunch of garbage cans right next to the rear entrance to one of the buildings, about five feet from the stain. The door was set back a little, so there was a shadowy alcove that would've been perfect for hiding if you wanted to shoot somebody.

The police must've noticed this.

I thought that, but I also knew that they—meaning Detective Culhane—had pretty much already convicted Miss Giddings. I couldn't recall him poking around the place where I was crouching down now, crawling around next to the trash cans.

It didn't seem that whoever owned them made much garbage, because there was snow on top of the metal lids, and the drifts near the alcove weren't disturbed either.

I edged a little closer and peeked into the shadowy spot, only to discover that the snow just outside the door *was* tramped down. And I also saw a very small object smushed into what looked like a footprint.

Although what I'd discovered may or may not have been a clue—or clues—my heart started racing like crazy, which is probably why I nearly jumped out of my skin when somebody asked me, in a bossy, snooty tone, "Why in the world are you *crawling around in garbage,* kid?"

CHAPTER 22

I DIDN'T APPRECIATE BEING CALLED "KID" BY ANOTHER child—although at least the girl in the blue velvet coat and fancy beret didn't call me "son" or "boy," like had happened too often lately.

"Are you pretending you're an alley cat or something?" she asked me, her hands on her hips. "Because that is a *terrible* game."

"I'm . . ." I started to inform Miss High-and-Mighty that I was on a practically official detective mission, to help a woman *in prison*, when all of a sudden I realized who she was. "Hey!" I cried, standing up and brushing snow off my knees. "You're Flora!"

She narrowed her blue eyes at me. "How do you know my name?"

"You're the Bakery Pride Bread girl," I said, only to realize that didn't explain why I knew her real name. "Plus, I saw you in the *Tribune* today. With your . . ."

I stopped myself before I said "father," because it finally struck me that this alley was the last place Flora Bessemer should be. We were standing right next to a bloodstain left by her dad.

"What are you doing here?" I asked, trying to move in front of that mark and block her view. But it was too late. She was staring at it. For a second, I didn't know what to do, and I prepared myself for when she would burst into big sobs, which is what I would've done.

And so I was very surprised when Flora Bessemer raised those blue eyes to meet mine again and I saw that she wasn't about to cry. Her lips were pursed, and her chin was jutting out, and her little mittened hands were balled into fists, but she wasn't fighting back tears. No . . . she looked like she was ready to fight a *person*. Punch somebody's lights out. Her blond corkscrew curls, peeking out from under her French-style hat, were quivering with rage.

"Are you okay?" I asked, hoping that the person about to get pounded wasn't me. I took a step back. "You look really mad!"

"My father just got murdered in cold blood," Flora informed me through gritted teeth. "You bet I'm mad!"

"I know." I raised my hands. "I was there."

That was probably the wrong thing to say. Flora balled her fists harder and lurched forward, like *I* was the killer. "What?"

"I was the first person there—after it all happened," I clarified. Then, although I wasn't sure it was a good idea, I added, "Except for Miss Giddings, of course."

Flora simmered down a little and gave me a curious look. "You know her?"

"Yeah. She's a nice lady." I started defending Miss Giddings, although I honestly couldn't tell how Flora felt about her. I glanced down at the blood. "She didn't do this, you know."

Flora gave me a level stare. Jeez, she was a tough kid, in spite of those curls. How did she look so sweet in those bread advertisements? "No, I don't know that," she said. "All I know is, she was the last person seen with my father."

I was going to point out that Flora's dad was a gangster, but if she didn't know that, it wasn't the right time to tell her. And if she did know it . . . Well, she probably knew all about how gangsters had enemies and killed each other all the time. She might even have her own suspicions about who'd gunned down her father—which I would be very interested in hearing sometime. For now, I just asked, "Well . . . do you *like* her? Miss Giddings?"

I could tell that Flora Bessemer and I weren't meant to be good friends. I didn't like the way she kept looking me up and down and wrinkling her pert, upturned nose, as if my secondhand clothes weren't good enough for her. But I did kind of admire the way she said, honestly and with less anger, "I don't know." She shrugged. "She seems okay." Her cheeks got red, as if she was getting mad again. "Sometimes I think she just wanted my father's money, though. He bought her a lot of things."

"Well, she certainly wouldn't have killed him then, right?" I reasoned. "If he was giving her presents?"

Flora crossed her arms and cocked her head. "I didn't *say* Miss Giddings . . . *did it,* did I?"

Now that she wasn't outright furious, she couldn't seem to bring herself to say "killed."

"Why are you here?" I asked again.

Flora could've asked me the same thing, but she probably didn't care who I was or what I did. She hadn't even asked my name. But she did answer the question, in a cold voice that scared me more than her anger. "I want to find out who murdered my father. And I want that person to pay. I came here to see where it happened, and to vow revenge."

Wow. She was *definitely* a gangster's daughter.

"Umm . . . have you vowed yet?" I asked, thinking maybe I should leave. Maybe "vowing" was something you needed to do alone.

Apparently she was already done. "My uncle is waiting," she said. Her gaze drifted to the bloodstain, and her cheeks got a little pale. I was pretty sure that she wasn't just angry. She was grieving, too. Maybe anger was how she mourned. Sometimes I got mad at my father, which wasn't fair at all. She met my gaze again. "I'm going now."

"See ya . . ."

Flora wasn't listening. She turned on her patent-leather heel and strode down the alley, head held high and curls bouncing.

I noticed, finally, an automobile at the end of the street. A sleek black sedan, against which a man was leaning. A huge guy in an overcoat, his arms crossed over his chest. When Flora reached the car, he straightened up and opened the back door.

She disappeared inside, and Flora's uncle made a point of staring at me for what felt like twenty minutes.

I got the sense I was getting a warning, but I didn't know why.

Then he got into the front seat and the sedan drove away, leaving me alone in the alley, trying to figure out what I should do with the might-be-clues I'd found—and how I could get a snippy, rich, but very tough girl on my side, fighting to keep Miss Giddings from the noose.

Because I sure didn't want Flora working *against* me, Miss Giddings, and Robert.

Then I thought about Flora's vow, and the large man who'd stared at me, and the fact that murder seemed like a way of life for her—not a big surprise, or anything to cry about—and wondered what I'd be getting myself into if we really did team up.

A world of trouble, probably.

CHAPTER 23

I SAT AT MY KITCHEN TABLE, GNAWING ON A PENCIL INSTEAD of eating the Wonder Bread with grape jelly I'd made for supper. Then I wrote down my first observation in an old composition book I'd kept from second grade.

Doorway in alley—snow tramped down right outside door. Would person have been near enough to Mr. Bessemer to shoot him "at close range"?

Taking a moment to picture the scene again, I made another note.

No footprints leading from doorway!

Then I resumed chewing what was left of my pencil's eraser, which was a poor substitute for most gum—not counting the disgusting kind that adults chewed when they had queasy stomachs. I'd found a piece of that on the doorstep, in a frozen glob, like somebody'd spit it out into the wrapper, tossed it down, and stepped on it.

Getting a little excited, I wrote,

Chewed up, squished down piece of Beeman's Original pepsin gum—NOT covered with snow.

"Isabel, where's your money for today?" my mother asked, just when it seemed that I might be onto something important. I would've been mad if I hadn't suddenly realized that I was in big trouble. "Did you put it in the jar?" Mom added. "Because it doesn't seem like there's more this evening."

My mother always knew to the penny how much was in that jar, and there was no sense in trying to pretend that I'd added my share for the day. I looked up to see her buttoning her wool coat, her head down, so at least she wouldn't notice me cringing with guilt when I half fibbed. "I didn't sell enough to make any money today."

Because I was running around pretending I was Detective Culhane—or a star crime reporter.

Mom raised her face, and all at once I felt sick to *my* stomach. Honestly, I could've gone for some pepsin gum. Though I might've been helping Miss Giddings, I'd clearly let my family down. "Really, Isabel?" Mom asked. "Nothing?"

She didn't sound angry. Just disappointed.

"Sorry." My cheeks got warm, which always happened when I wasn't exactly honest. "It was a really cold day, and nobody was stopping . . ."

My mother resumed buttoning her coat, getting ready for work, and it struck me how rough her hands looked, no doubt from cleaning. Her hair — naturally frizzy, like mine — was showing some gray, too, and she was getting wrinkles around her eyes. Not from laughing, either.

"I'll work double hard tomorrow," I promised. "I'm sure I can make up for today."

"It's not your fault, Isabel," Mom reassured me, so I felt even more guilty. "You can't force people to buy newspapers."

No, I couldn't. But I could at least stay at my corner.

My mother came over to the table and turned her head sideways, trying to see my composition book. "What are you writing?"

I pulled the book closer to myself, blocking her view. She would definitely ask questions if she read the words *shoot* and *at close range*, not to mention a strange man's name. And given that I wasn't a very good liar, it probably wouldn't be long before I spilled the beans about being kind of involved in a murder and getting questioned at a police station.

"It's nothing," I said, placing my hand over my notes. "Just stupid ideas I have."

Mom stepped back so she could meet my eyes. "Don't

ever say that, Isabel. You've always had a talent for writing, just like your father." She frowned. "And maybe someday—"

She was going to say that maybe someday I'd go back to school, but we both knew that probably wouldn't happen, at least not any time soon, and I interrupted her, closing the notebook. "You want me to make you a sandwich or something? To take with you?"

"No, thanks." Mom leaned over, squeezed my shoulder, and kissed the top of my head. "Keep the door locked, and don't let anybody in."

"Okay," I said. "I'll lock up."

My mother left then, and I was glad she hadn't said anything about me staying home, because a few minutes after she was gone, I did lock the door—but behind me, so I could keep one more promise I'd made the night before. A pledge I *had* to keep, even though, when I stepped outside, I suddenly realized that I wasn't exactly sure where I was going.

CHAPTER 24

I EXPECTED ONE OF TWO SURPRISES WHEN I FOUND ROBERT Giddings's house again.

Either I'd be *good* surprised to find him at home or I'd be *bad* surprised to find the house empty. I didn't know where his aunt lived, and—though I'd found a shortcut so the walk from my house wasn't as bad as the first time —it was still freezing outside. I really wanted a chance to warm up.

I never, ever expected the shock I actually got when somebody, thank goodness, did open the door, swinging it wide so I could see the whole parlor.

"Jeez, Louise!" I blurted. "What are *you* doing here?"

CHAPTER 25

SABEL, WHAT IN THE WORLD . . ." MAUDE COLLIER SOUNDED confused—even a little worried—as she stepped back and started to ask why I'd shown up at Robert Giddings's house when most kids were getting ready for bed.

But Detective Culhane seemed—big surprise—irritated to see me enter the cozy parlor. He crossed his arms, demanding, "Why are you here—again?"

"I told Robert I'd check on him," I informed them both, looking from one to the other until I almost got dizzy. Maude was settling into the floral chair where I'd sat the night before, opening her notebook, and Detective Culhane stood in the middle of the pretty hooked rug.

Are they teaming up against a poor, crippled kid?

Because that would be really wrong.

Then I noticed Hastings warming himself by a radiator and brightened up a little. "Hey, Detective Hastings! How are you?"

"Why, I'm just . . ." Poor Hastings started to answer, then glanced at Detective Culhane and muttered "fine" without meeting my eyes again.

Apparently, talking to me was against the rules or something.

"Isabel, this is not a good time." Detective Culhane moved toward me, as if he was going to grab my arm and toss me out, but I stomped the snow off my boots and sidestepped him. I'd finally gotten a good look at Robert. He was lying very still on the sofa, under a blanket, and his face was even more pale than usual. In fact, I'd been so surprised to see Maude, who was sitting close to him, that I'd almost overlooked him.

"Robert, are you okay?" I asked. Before he could answer, I turned and glared at Maude and Detective Culhane, my fists balled up like I was Flora Bessemer, itching to fight. "Are they bothering you?"

"Isabel, calm down," Maude urged in a soothing voice. "Don't make things worse."

"What's bad to start with?" I asked, looking around at everybody.

That was when, out of the corner of my eye, I noticed the gun on the coffee table.

CHAPTER 26

WHY IS *THAT* HERE?" I ASKED, POINTING AT THE GUN—
which was pointing back at *me*. Nobody was holding it, but somehow that didn't make it much less scary.
Probably because I'd seen that hole in Charles Bessemer's head not too long ago. I looked at Detective Culhane. "Is that *the*—"

"It's time for you to leave, Miss Feeney," he said, cutting me off. He took my shoulder and started guiding me to the door. Twisting, I slipped free. "Isabel . . ."

"Robert, what's going on?" I demanded, addressing the ghost that hovered under the blanket. The *bluish* ghost. "Are you cold or something? What's wrong?"

"I'm okay, Isabel," he reassured me. But his voice was soft and wheezy. "Sometimes the cold bothers me if I go out too much—like to my aunt's." He paused to get some air. "It gets hard to breathe. It's from having polio, you know . . . It happens to a lot of kids . . ."

So Robert really had survived polio. I could hardly

imagine that, although the disease scared the bejeepers out of me every summer. Some people said that if you ate peach fuzz, you'd get it. Which really made things difficult for me because I loved a good peach.

"Miss Feeney." Detective Culhane spoke firmly—and used my last name again—so I knew I was going to get kicked out and miss whatever the heck was happening.

Then, just as I was turning to go, Maude surprised me, saying quietly, "James. Why don't you let Isabel stay? You're almost done here, and I think Robert could use a friend." She rested one hand on Robert's shoulder, addressing him. "You'd probably like some company your own age, right?"

Robert nodded. "Yes. Please."

Maude didn't say anything else. She just turned her dark, confident eyes on stone-faced James Culhane, and the second I looked at him, I knew she was going to get her way. He didn't melt like a snowman in August, but his shoulders slumped, just a little. "Fine," he agreed through gritted teeth. "She can stay."

Wow. Either he *really* liked her or Maude Collier was just a woman who got what she wanted. It was probably a little of both.

I looked at Maude, mouthing, *Thanks*.

She winked at me, and I once again wasn't sure if we were friends or enemies in this whole mess.

Could we be both?

Then, because I knew Detective Culhane's rules for

me—sit still and shut up—I climbed onto the pretty high-backed chair that matched Maude's and buttoned my lips. I actually made a buttoning motion, so he'd know I understood what was expected of me.

Detective Culhane was already done with me, though. He was pulling the rocking chair across the floor and sitting down close to Robert, so they were more on the same level. Then he reached to the coffee table that was between them and picked up the gun. "You are certain that you can't tell me if this was your mother's or not?" he asked. "Because she is having a very difficult time identifying it too."

Detective Culhane obviously believed that Miss Giddings was not really having trouble at all.

Meanwhile, *I* believed Robert when he shook his head, his eyes wide behind his glasses. "No," he choked out. "I swear. I told you. She never let me touch it!"

"Plus, all guns kinda look the same, don't they?" I interjected.

Detective Culhane turned slowly to me. "No, Miss Feeney. They do not." He kept staring at me, as if he was waiting for something. I finally figured out what, and buttoned my lip again. He turned back to Robert. "Why did she have a gun? Where did it come from?"

Robert stared down at his covered-up legs. *Why isn't he at his aunt's house?* I wondered. Then he picked at the blanket, muttering, "It was my father's. He left it behind when *he* left."

I really wished I could see Robert's face better, because he sounded not just polio sick, but heartsick and bitter all at the same time.

Was Robert angry at his father? Was his dad still *alive?*

I glanced at the mantel and noticed that there weren't any pictures of a man there. My mother kept three photographs of Dad in our small parlor. And she had their wedding picture next to her bed.

Had there been any photographs like that next to Miss Giddings's bed?

And why, now that I thought of it, was she *Miss* Giddings?

My mother still went by *Mrs.* Feeney . . .

"James." Maude's quiet voice interrupted my thoughts. I turned to see that Hastings was sneaking in a nap, right on his feet, now that he was behind Detective Culhane, out of his boss's sight. Then I noted that Maude was frowning, and for a second, I thought she was going to step in to help Robert again. Maybe tell Detective Culhane that he'd upset a frail, wheezing kid enough for one night. But that didn't happen. Instead, she asked, "Were Miss Giddings's fingerprints on the *trigger?*"

I was starting to learn that being a reporter meant you couldn't always be kind. That sometimes you had to ask hard questions, even if some kid was under a blanket struggling to breathe.

Could I really do that job?

"No, but she could have started to wipe the gun clean," Detective Culhane said. "She had plenty of time to do that before the police came."

Maude shifted to meet my eyes. "Isabel, did you see anything?"

"No. She wasn't cleaning the gun when I got there!" I cried, grateful to finally be allowed to talk. "I swear!"

Of course, Detective Culhane wasn't impressed, although he did speak to me almost like I was a human being. "You weren't there right away, Isabel. You told us that you had to run from the corner."

"Yes, but . . ." That was true, but I had more to say. "I found this footprint . . . And a doorway . . ." I started to pull my composition book out of my coat, which I was still wearing, since nobody'd suggested I take it off. "And trash cans with lids . . . and gum . . ." The stuff I'd found in the alley had made some sense to me, even if I hadn't pieced everything together yet, but sitting there with Detective Culhane staring at me, I found myself babbling. I tried to appeal to Maude, who was watching me with her head cocked, clearly confused, which didn't help me sort out my thoughts. "Gum . . ." I said weakly, holding up my notes. "I found this gum—"

"We are talking about *guns,* Miss Feeney," Detective Culhane interrupted. "With an *n.* Not *gum,* with an *m.*"

"Hey," I snapped, getting mad. "I might not go to school anymore, but I know how to spell! I'm not stupid!"

That woke up Hastings, even. He grunted and snorted, and his eyes flew open—while Detective Culhane reared back in his chair, as if I'd hit him. There was a big silence, and I thought he was going to really give it to me. Maybe pick me up and toss me out in the snow.

But that didn't happen. Instead, he got a funny look on his face. "I'm sorry, Isabel," he said. "I didn't mean to imply anything like that."

What?

I probably should've told him that it was okay. That I accepted his apology. But I was so stunned that I just sat there, until Maude finally spoke, in her quiet way that somehow worked better than my loud outbursts. "James, I think it's time we let Robert rest. Is there really anything else you can learn here?"

"I suppose not," he agreed, still watching me. Just when I was getting uncomfortable, he stood up and asked Hastings, "Are you awake enough to deliver Robert to his aunt?" He jerked his thumb at me. "Then take her home?"

Did Detective Culhane see *everything?* Did he have eyes in the back of his head? I was sure he hadn't turned around once to catch Hastings napping and that he'd been completely focused on me, Robert, and Maude.

Beleaguered old Hastings didn't try to pretend he'd been awake. And I liked him even better when he walked over to the couch and held out his arms. "Come on, pal. You look like you need a ride."

But Robert shook his head. "No. I'll stay here." He glanced at me. "I have to stay here."

"No, it's okay," I told him, thinking he felt that he had to stick around because I'd come to visit. "I'll come back again."

But Robert wasn't staying for me. He picked at the blanket again. "No, it's not that."

"Robert . . ."

I looked over to see that Maude, who was near the door putting on her coat, wasn't being a reporter right then. She was just a nice lady worried about a sick kid. "Why not stay with your aunt?" she asked.

Robert kept shredding his blanket. "It's not good for me to go outside. I told you. And she shares a house with some other ladies. There's no room for me. She'd rather just take care of me here. She'll probably be here soon. She said she'd be late."

"I really don't mind carrying you," Hastings offered again. He smiled. "I bet those ladies at the boarding house would like to help you out until your aunt can take over."

"No!"

We were all surprised by how he barked at us. "Robert?" Maude asked uncertainly.

Robert finally raised his face, and I saw two small pink blotches on his cheeks. He wasn't feeling better, though. He was angry. "I *can't* go to my aunt's, okay?"

Maude gave Detective Culhane a worried, confused look, then asked, "Why not?"

I was pretty sure that Robert—who probably didn't go to school either—was as smart as I was, if not smarter. But he obviously didn't always think before he spoke, at least around police, and Detective Culhane nearly dropped the gun that he was slipping into a big tan envelope when Robert said, "Aunt Johnene says she's not disrupting *her* 'respectable' house with the mess Mom made, because she knew Mom would get into some kind of trouble!"

CHAPTER 27

WHAT IS WRONG WITH YOU?" I ASKED ROBERT AFTER THE adults had left—without me, although I'd *really* wanted that ride. But how could I leave a breathless, upset, and for once *too talkative* kid alone? "Did that polio get your brain or something?"

Robert jerked upright. "Hey!"

I didn't apologize for mentioning his disease. I felt sorry for Robert, but I didn't understand why people always pretended they didn't even notice the bad stuff that happened to you. He'd had polio, for crying out loud, and not talking about it wasn't going to change anything. Just like everybody avoiding talking about my dad wouldn't make him any less dead.

"Why did you say that about your mom?" I groaned, plopping down on the rocking chair Detective Culhane had just been using—and the chair tried to kick me out too, like he'd left it with orders. I got it steadied and asked, again, "Honestly, why?"

Robert shrugged his bony shoulders. "I don't know. I just got angry."

"At your aunt or your mom?"

Robert started plucking at threads again. "Both."

"I am gonna rip that blanket off you if you don't leave it alone," I warned him. "You are making me crazy!"

Robert stilled his hands and gave me sad eyes. "Why are you being so mean tonight? I thought we were . . ."

Friends.

I avoided saying the word too. Was that because we were so used to not having any? But I did simmer down. "Sorry. My mom says I get 'wrought up' easy. I just don't understand why you'd give Detective Culhane and Maude—"

Robert gave me a funny look. "Maude?"

"Yeah." I didn't feel like explaining *that* complicated relationship, so I turned the conversation back to the stupid thing Robert had just said. "I don't understand why you'd give them more reason to think your mother's guilty."

Robert's eyes got wide. "Did I do that?"

I gave *him* a weird look. "Uh . . . yeah."

What he'd just done finally seemed to sink in. I settled back in the chair. "Why would your aunt think your mom would get in trouble?"

"Aunt Johnene didn't like Mr. Bessemer. She said he was bad news."

"Yeah, I guess he was."

I glanced at a clock on the mantel. It was pretty late. "Your aunt's not coming tonight, is she?"

Robert opened his mouth, as if he was going to lie to me; then his shoulders slumped. "No. Probably not. She does come, but not that often." He turned pleading eyes on me. "Please don't tell anybody I'm alone a lot. They might put me in an orphanage or something!"

"I . . . I'm alone a lot too," I confided, something I wasn't supposed to tell anyone. Mom sometimes worried that I'd get taken away if people knew how often I was on my own. "I'll keep your secret," I promised. "You don't tell anybody about me, either, right?"

Robert nodded. "Okay."

We both got quiet, and I rocked back and forth, thinking. Then I asked a question that wouldn't stop bugging me. It was a nosy one, but if I was going to be a reporter, I'd better get used to poking around in people's business. "So, if Mr. Bessemer was so terrible, why did your mom want to marry him?"

Robert was looking better now that Detective Culhane was gone, as if the cold wasn't the only thing that had sucked the breath out of him, but he actually got pink when I asked that. "I think . . . I think she was going to marry him partly because of me," he said. Then he paused, swallowing thickly, before adding, "You know . . . because of what I did to my father."

I stopped rocking and stared at him.

What the heck did *that* mean?

CHAPTER 28

FOR A SPLIT SECOND I THOUGHT ROBERT HAD KILLED HIS dad—and maybe murdered Charles Bessemer, too. I had no idea how a kid who dragged one leg and could barely breathe sometimes would get himself and a gun to a dark alley, but what he'd just said . . . well, it sounded pretty darn ominous.

"You should probably explain all that," I suggested, scooching the chair out of arm's reach. He was making me a little nervous. "What, exactly, did you do?"

But Robert hadn't been talking about hurting anybody. He was the one who'd gotten hurt. He just *blamed* himself. "My father thought I was a weakling even before I got polio," he said. "And then he thought I didn't fight *that* hard enough. He thought a stronger son would've been able to walk normally again."

That was the craziest thing I'd ever heard. "Your father sounds like a bully!"

Robert just shrugged. "Anyway, he and Mom fought

all the time after I got sick. She kept telling him to leave me alone, and he kept saying he couldn't stand having a kid everybody pitied. Then, one day, he left, and we started acting like he'd never existed."

Robert's voice sounded funny, and I realized he was crying. Which was probably behavior his dad wouldn't have liked either.

"Gosh, Robert, I'm sorry." I didn't know what else to say. I almost wished he'd be more like Flora Bessemer and get mad and vow vengeance. That was actually easier to handle. "But what's that have to do with your mom and Charles Bessemer?"

"My mother never said it to me, but I'm pretty sure she was going to marry him because he was the first man who didn't run away when he met me."

"What's *that* mean?"

"You know how pretty my mom is." Robert said that as if it were a bad thing. "A lot of men ask her out on dates," he continued glumly. "But whenever they meet me, they all stop calling." He forced a weak smile. "Who wants to get stuck with a crippled kid, right?"

I still liked Miss Giddings, but it seemed as if she did have terrible taste in men. Or maybe most men were just terrible.

I felt extra proud of my father, who wouldn't have turned his back on a lame boy. I mean, I hadn't really known my dad, who'd died when I was very little, but my mother always told me stories about what a good man he was. I was also suddenly glad that my mom hadn't brought around a bunch of horrible potential fathers. Maybe her going gray wasn't such a bad thing after all.

"So Mr. Bessemer liked you?" I asked. "Was nice to you?"

Robert was done crying. He wiped his nose with the sleeve of his pajamas, then shook his head. "Nah. He didn't really pay any attention to me either way." Robert rolled his eyes. "He was always too busy fussing over *Flora* and her commercials and acting to even notice me."

"Hey, I met her!" I said.

"Lucky you," Robert grumbled, not even asking how or where. He was too caught up in his own story. "Mr. Bessemer had money, too," he added. "Mom thought that was a good thing."

"You're not supposed to marry for money!" Even I knew that. Had I been wrong about Miss Giddings after all?

"Not for *herself*," Robert clarified. "I overheard Mom tell Aunt Johnene that Mr. Bessemer could afford treatment that might help me walk right again."

I didn't believe that such a treatment existed. But Miss Giddings would probably always hope—and do anything to get Robert help. Maybe even marry somebody she didn't love as much as she should.

"I think Mom really believed he'd be a good husband, too," Robert noted, as if he were reading my mind. "Because—even if he wasn't always perfect toward her, and had a temper—he *could* be nice, and he mainly treated her well . . ."

Robert was talking faster, but his breathing was getting ragged again.

"I understand," I promised him. "Really."

He nodded. "Okay."

"You should rest," I suggested. "Just for a couple minutes."

Nodding again, he closed his eyes, and I didn't think a full sixty seconds passed before he was breathing steadier, because he was sound asleep. All the stuff he was going through—and had been through—must've worn him out.

I wanted to leave and get some sleep myself, but I sat in the rocking chair watching him almost all night. It just seemed that, for once in his life, somebody besides his mother ought to really stick by him.

Okay, maybe I dozed off once or twice, like Hastings, with my chin on my chest. For the most part, though, I hovered over Robert Giddings like a dog protecting a bone.

And when the sun started to come up, I shook his shoulder and woke him up enough to say goodbye, then ran home before Mom got back from the hospital.

Soon after that, it was time for *me* to go to work. But when I got to my corner, somebody else was already standing there.

Waiting, I was pretty sure, for me.

CHAPTER 29

MISS GIDDINGS WAS MOVIE-STAR PRETTY, BUT SOMETHING about Maude Collier drew your attention, even when she just stood on a corner with her hands in the pockets of a tailored tweed coat, watching everything around her with a half smile, as if the whole city amused her.

She looked like she owned Chicago—which, in a way, I guess she did.

Could I ever look that confident?

"Hey, Maude," I greeted her, dumping some of my papers onto the ground and immediately starting to sell the ones in my arms. Some of my regular customers were passing by, and we did our usual ritual of me handing them a *Trib* and them shoving coins into my palm, which didn't prevent me from talking. "Why are you here?"

"I visited Miss Giddings in prison yesterday," she said. "And I wrote an article based on our talk—"

"Hey, Mr. Forebush!" I handed one of my regulars a paper and took my cash. Then I turned back to Maude. "And . . ."

Maude's eyes clouded over. "I don't think you'll like it, Isabel. I wanted to warn you because I think you'll be upset with me."

I froze like a statue, my hand out to accept some coins. And although part of me really wanted to know what was in that story, I first had to ask, "You . . . you came here because you're worried I'll be *mad* at you?"

"Yes, Isabel," Maude confirmed, sidestepping. The sidewalk was pretty crowded with men and women, all bundled against the cold. "We're friends, right?"

Were we?

I honestly didn't know how to answer, but I did think it was pretty nice . . . okay, *unbelievable* . . . that Chicago's most famous lady reporter had come to see *me*. Still, I was loyal to Miss Giddings—and now Robert. "What's in the story?" I asked warily.

I admired but didn't always like Maude Collier—and I'd probably like her less in a few minutes—but how *couldn't* I think she was the bee's knees when she said with a grin, "Hand me those *Trib*s, Izzie. I'll sell while you read."

CHAPTER 30

"PRETTIEST" KILLER: MAYBE GUN WAS MINE!

by Maude Collier

Colette Giddings, discovered in an alley wearing a fur coat stained by the blood of the abusive man who'd bought it for her, today told detectives she "can't recall" if the gun found next to her fiancé's body is the one she recently denied owning.

"All guns look alike to me," she said with a pout. "I don't like them!"

And yet Giddings, dubbed the "prettiest woman on Murderess's Row," has admitted that she earlier lied about having a small pistol, which she kept bedside.

The gun, she still insists, really belonged to the man she divorced, Albert Rowland, of late employed at Swift's Meats . . .

I looked up from reading Maude's article, my head swirling with all kinds of thoughts and feelings I couldn't sort out.

First of all, Robert's father suddenly had a name. Albert. And a different last name. Rowland. Not to mention a job—at a butcher shop not far from where Maude and I were standing. I passed it every day.

Had I ever *seen* Robert's dad?

And Maude . . . she'd once again made Miss Giddings look guilty—even worse than before. She'd also made it seem like Miss Giddings had left Albert Rowland, when I knew it was the other way around.

Yet she'd not only come to see me, a nobody kid, to make sure I didn't get too upset, she was smiling and hawking my newspapers. And selling way more than I did, because pretty much every man who passed by bought one, then looked over his shoulder at her as he walked away.

Talk about an unfair advantage!

And an unfair article.

But I was starting to understand the reporter side of the newspaper business. I also—finally—got that my being mad wouldn't change the way Maude wrote about Miss Giddings.

No—if I was going to get Maude to tell a different story, I'd have to make her believe a different story.

"Hey, Maude," I said, giving her the newspaper I held so she could sell that, too. "When you're done filling up my mom's money jar, you wanna go see that murder scene? The way *I* see it?"

CHAPTER 31

DO YOU WANNA BORROW MY BOOTS?" I OFFERED, WATCH-ing Maude step carefully through the snow toward the garbage cans where Flora'd caught me snooping. Maude's high heels were not meant for ice and slush, and she'd fallen behind. "The boots are pretty big. I could toss 'em to you."

Maude just laughed and kept picking her way through some deep, dirty ruts. By now, more traffic—auto and foot—had come down the alley. But the spot where I stood was still undisturbed, except for my footprints.

"And what would *you* do, Isabel?" Maude asked, still grinning. "Stand barefoot in the snow?"

I hadn't thought that through. "We could trade. I could wear your shoes."

Like I'd be able to even stand on those heels.

"Thanks, but I'm fine," Maude promised. "I've walked through worse messes than this to get a story."

Immediately, I was curious. "Like what?"

"Well . . ." She stopped walking for a moment. "I've trudged through the ash-covered remains of big fires. And waded into the river to get a better look when a corpse was being dredged out. And of course, I've stepped over bodies, sometimes several at once, because this *is* a violent city."

I knew it was strange, but oh, how I envied the way Maude could talk about those things as if they were commonplace. What other woman could claim to have witnessed so much?

Maude took the last few steps to meet me and didn't bother brushing snow off of her pretty red-leather shoes. She just pulled her ever-present notebook and pencil out of her pocket. "So, Isabel," she said, "tell me what you see here that strikes you as important."

I felt a little silly at first, but I took out my composition book, too, and said, "Okay. Here goes."

CHAPTER 32

S O YOU FOUND FOOTPRINTS LEADING OUT A DOOR—AND going nowhere." Maude summarized the things I'd just told her. We walked side-by-side out of the alley. "And the person wasn't taking out the trash," she continued. "Because there was—is—undisturbed snow on the lids."

I nodded, glad that she seemed to be taking me seriously. "Yeah."

Maude checked her notebook. "And the pepsin gum, which someone stepped on—after it snowed . . ."

"Yeah, that too." I studied her face. "Do you think it's important?"

We stopped under the streetlamp where I'd first seen Charles Bessemer, and she frowned at me. "I don't know, Isabel. It's not much."

I defended my findings. "It's something. Clues that maybe Detective Culhane didn't notice, because he was already so sure Miss Giddings was guilty." I looked at Maude even closer, narrowing my eyes. "How come you were with him at Robert's last night? Where were the other reporters?"

"That was a coincidence," she said. "*You* led me to Robert. James just happened to show up at the same time." Her cheeks got pink, and not only from the cold. "I also hound him for information when I'm covering a case he's on. He might have mentioned going there to talk about the gun."

It was the first time I'd seen Maude Collier, self-assured reporter, look even slightly flushed and flustered, and it was my turn to laugh at her. "Jeez, why don't you two just get married or something!"

All of a sudden she got serious. "James was married, before the war. His wife died in the terrible influenza epidemic while he was overseas." She looked down the street, distracted. "It's complicated, Isabel."

Yeah, I guess it was. I could hardly believe that Detective Culhane had been in love once. And now I also understood why he was so somber. "Sorry," I said. "I didn't mean to laugh."

Maude met my eyes again. "And I didn't mean to burden a young girl with all that." She smiled. "I think you *will* be a reporter, Isabel, if you can get that much information out of people with just a joking question!"

For the first time ever, I felt that my dream honestly might come true—and that, while we didn't always agree, Maude and I really had become friends. Something had changed in the way we'd just talked, almost like we were equals. But friendship or no friendship, I still didn't exactly understand why she saw Miss Giddings one way and I saw her another.

Which is why I came up with my most brilliant idea ever.

"Hey, Maude," I said. "I have a deal for you."

She raised one dark eyebrow, as if she was skeptical —and amused. "And what would that be, Izzie?"

"You take me to see Miss Giddings tomorrow, we'll both talk to her, and we'll *both* write stories based on the interview."

Maude was definitely intrigued. "And . . ."

"If my story's good enough"—I gave it a title, running my hand across the air—"'"Prettiest" Inmate Talks to Crime Scene Newsgirl,' you'll convince the *Tribune* to run it!"

CHAPTER 33

THE COOK COUNTY JAIL, ON HUBBARD STREET, WAS EVEN more intimidating than the Tribune Tower. The prison wasn't as tall or as majestic as the Tower — in fact, it was squat and ugly — but it looked like a gloomy castle that might house a king who'd lop your head off for no good reason.

I was just about to turn around, thinking I could tell Maude, who was late, that the deal I'd fought so hard for was probably stupid, when I felt a tap on my shoulder and jumped about a mile. And when I spun around, Chicago's most famous lady reporter, who'd been in that jail a thousand times, was laughing at me. It must've been really obvious that I was having second thoughts — which was why, of course, I had to say, as if I could hardly wait to get inside, "You ready to convince them to let a kid visit Murderess's Row?"

CHAPTER 34

MAUDE, I DON'T KNOW ABOUT LETTING A GIRL IN HERE . . ."
The guard who watched the desk just inside the prison's big double doors didn't look mean. On the contrary, Morse—that's what his name tag said—seemed a little nervous himself.

"Isabel will be perfectly safe with me," Maude promised, resting one gloved hand on my shoulder. "You know that I am very familiar with this place and its residents."

"Plus, I'm on official *Tribune* business," I pointed out, stretching the truth just a tiny bit—and probably pushing things way too far by adding, "You don't want to make the publisher of the city's biggest newspaper mad, right? 'Cause he's counting on my story."

Morse looked cockeyed at my escort. "That true, Maude?" He jerked a thumb at me. "This *kid* works for the *Trib*?"

The nice thing was, Maude didn't even have to lie, because I *did* work for the paper. "She sure does, Danny."

The guard still seemed skeptical, but before we had to keep arguing, somebody behind us said, "Let them in, Morse."

Maude and I both turned to see Detective Culhane standing there, his arms crossed, watching our whole exchange. I was just about to ask why the heck he wanted me to get involved in the investigation—did he finally want my help?—when he answered my questions. "I'm afraid," he noted, "that letting Isabel Feeney see the inside of a prison is the only way to *possibly* keep her out of one in the future."

I started to stick my tongue out at him, then realized that might land me in jail as more than a visitor, like he'd just predicted. I also grasped that what he'd just done, for whatever reason, had *worked*.

I was actually going to see Murderess's Row.

CHAPTER 35

WHENEVER MAUDE WROTE ABOUT LADIES' LIVES IN prison, she always made it seem as if things were pretty nice. Sometimes she even called Murderess's Row a "spa," where women who committed crimes could relax and work on their appearance while they waited to go on trial.

But the place looked gloomy to me. Sure, a lot of the women we passed—most of whom greeted Maude by name—weren't necessarily in cells. A surprising number were wandering around, busy with chores that looked less difficult than selling newspapers in the freezing cold. Some carried stacks of laundry, and some mopped the floor. Those who were behind bars were mostly occupied too, with sewing or reading. I wouldn't have minded spending all day with a book. Still, everything was gray and ugly, and there were plenty of bars to make a person feel trapped, so I wouldn't have called it someplace to take a vacation.

And reading a bunch of Maude's articles certainly didn't prepare me for what I saw when she stopped in front of a cell and said, "Hey, Colette. You've got *two* visitors today."

The woman inside was sitting on her cot, her back to us. And when she turned slowly to face me, I couldn't help crying out, "Miss Giddings! Holy cow!"

CHAPTER 36

WHERE'D ALL THE ROSES COME FROM?" I ASKED MISS GID-
dings after Maude and I had made ourselves kind
of at home in her boquet-filled cell. It had taken me
about ten minutes to reassure her that Robert was fine,
and another ten to explain why I was there, visiting the
most colorful spot in the jail. Compared with most of
the prison Miss Giddings's cell was hardly depressing at
all, except for the spare bed and the toilet and the gray
walls. Okay, maybe it was a little depressing. Still, the
flowers did cheer it up. "Who sent all these?"

Miss Giddings hadn't looked guilty when Detective
Culhane questioned her about the murder, but she looked
pretty uncomfortable over a simple inquiry about posies.
"It seems that I have some admirers"—she glanced at
Maude—"since my picture ran in the *Tribune.*"

I wanted to ask what kind of crazy men fell for a
woman who was accused of killing her last boyfriend,
but I couldn't think of a way to pose the question that

wouldn't insult Miss Giddings. Meanwhile, Maude, leaning against the bars, notebook discreetly in her left hand, didn't seem surprised. "It always happens," she said with a shrug. "Every time."

"I didn't ask for this attention," Miss Giddings said softly. I sensed that she was angry at Maude, but well aware that the reporter had all the power. It probably wouldn't help, and might hurt, to fight back about being called a "slayer" — even a "pretty" one — in a newspaper before she was tried. "I don't want these flowers."

Maude didn't respond, but she did make a note.

I took out my composition book too, although I wasn't sure if something important had just been said. Nothing had seemed worth noting to me. So I wrote down how Miss Giddings looked, which had made me cry out when I first saw her.

Still pretty, but pale. Red eyes. Crying?? Too skinny! Hair not shiny, but curls still better than mine. Dress like a paper sack!!

Looking up, I realized that Miss Giddings and Maude were both watching me. "Go ahead, Isabel," Maude urged. "Ask a question. You can't write a story without asking questions."

Maybe I wasn't destined to be a great reporter after all, because the first thing that popped into my mind—

and out of my mouth—was, "Hey, do you know anybody that chews that horrible Beeman's pepsin gum?"

Miss Giddings gave me a funny look, so I added, "You know, the kind that helps calm your stomach when you wanna upchuck?"

"I know what you mean, Izzie," Miss Giddings said, still with a strange expression on her face. "I'm just surprised by the question."

"Yeah, me too," I agreed. "But do you know anybody like that?"

Miss Giddings nodded. "Yes. In fact, I do."

All of a sudden I got excited, and I poised my pencil over my notes, ready to write—which I completely forgot to do when Miss Giddings shocked both me and Maude by saying, "My *husband*."

CHAPTER 37

I NEARLY FELL OFF THE COT WHEN MISS GIDDINGS SAID THAT this terrible man—who'd abandoned a son just because the kid had a paralyzed leg—chewed the very type of gum I'd found near a murder scene.

Maude, however, seemed mainly interested in the fact that Miss Giddings was still married. "I thought you were divorced," she said, her pencil scribbling. I saw her glance at Miss Giddings's ring finger, which was bare now, the big diamond missing. "And weren't you engaged?" Maude asked. "Because bigamy is a crime too."

She was making a joke, and needless to say, Miss Giddings didn't laugh. I shot Maude a look, trying to tell her to cut it out. But she was focused on Miss Giddings, who clearly realized that being engaged to a mobster while still married to some other man was probably going to look bad in the next day's newspaper. Her shoulders slumped. "Albert was just about to sign the final papers," she said. "At least, I was trying to get him to do that."

Her cheeks got red with indignation. "You don't know what it's like to deal with a stubborn, mean man like Albert Rowland." She looked at me. "That's why he always chews that gum. He's so bitter, it takes a toll on his stomach!" Then, though I wanted to talk more about Albert's indigestion, Miss Giddings turned back to Maude. "I consider us divorced. I just needed to convince him that it was time to make it official—"

"By warning him that your boyfriend, Charles Bessemer, was a mobster who might get angry, and perhaps violent, if those papers weren't signed?" Maude suggested.

Miss Giddings's cheeks got brighter red. "No! That's not true!" She cooled down and got quieter. "I simply told Albert that even if he couldn't accept having a crippled son, he could at least step aside and let me marry a man who could care for Robert."

I was just a kid, but once again I thought that seemed like a bad idea. But it wasn't my place to say—especially since I saw how my mother struggled alone to raise me, and I was *healthy*—so I stayed quiet until Miss Giddings turned to me and asked, "Why did you ask that, Izzie? About the gum?"

"I was crawling around the alley, looking for clues to find the *real* killer, when I found a piece squished in a footprint on top of the snow—"

"Izzie . . . you did that for me?" Miss Giddings's eyes

glistened, as if she might cry out of gratitude. "Please, don't get involved . . ."

"Oh, I'm involved," I promised. "And Flora Bessemer's getting in on the act too. She's vowed to find the killer—and kill him back!"

"What's this about Flora Bessemer?" Maude asked sharply. Suddenly *I* was getting interviewed. "You know her? And what's this vow?"

"Can we focus on the gum?" I asked, afraid that I shouldn't have mentioned Flora and her death oath. "Because it really seemed to me like somebody'd spit it out—"

"So you think Albert Rowland might've been jealous?" Maude asked. "Enough to hide in an alley and kill the man who was courting his wife?"

She seemed doubtful, but at least she hadn't dismissed the idea.

"Maybe," I said. "Maybe he even meant to shoot Miss Giddings and missed!"

Miss Giddings gasped and put her hand to her throat, her gaze darting between me and Maude. "Do you think . . ."

Maude arced a skeptical eyebrow, but I kept going. "It coulda happened that way! What if Albert Rowland realized he still loved you, Miss Giddings, and didn't want you to marry somebody else? What if he flew into a rage? You said he was mean!"

"Those are some interesting theories, Miss Feeney," said a voice from behind me.

Aw, horsefeathers! I looked outside the cell to find Detective Culhane watching me, as if I were a monkey in a zoo. I'd completely forgotten that he'd been spooking around the jail. "I can tell you don't think they're interesting at all," I advised him. "I can spell, and I get sarcasm, too."

I guess I hadn't exactly forgiven him for the "g-u-n" comment. Then I remembered how Detective Culhane had fought in a terrible war, and lost his wife, and how he had tried to feed me, once, and I felt bad for snapping at him.

"Sorry," I offered, without even being told to say it.

But the adults were already preoccupied. First, Maude and Detective Culhane shared a long look that erased any doubts I might've had about them being sweet on each other. But it was a sad look, too, like they had more than real bars between them. Then Detective Culhane spoke to Miss Giddings, who'd stood up and was nervously smoothing her baggy dress, as if she'd already learned that visits from a high-ranking cop weren't usually good news. And she was right. He told her solemnly, "The coroner's jury has determined that there is sufficient evidence to turn your case over for trial."

Miss Giddings staggered backwards and rested her hand on her chest. I stood up just in time to grab her arm in case she was about to faint dead away. "No . . ." she whispered, wide-eyed. "But . . ."

"Is there anything you want to tell me?" Detective Culhane pressed, while Maude took rapid-fire notes —which I could not do, since I was holding Miss Giddings. "Anything you'd like to say? Because this could go easier—"

He wanted a confession. "Don't let him bully you into saying something not true!" I warned Miss Giddings. "He's trying to scare you!"

Those bars might've been meant to keep people in, but when I looked at Detective Culhane, I was glad he was shut *out*. "Are you an attorney now, Miss Feeney?" he growled. "Are you Miss Giddings's legal counsel? Because if you are not, I strongly suggest that you—"

"I know, I know," I said, letting go of Miss Giddings and sinking down onto the cot. "Sit down and shut up."

"Yes," Detective Culhane said evenly. "Until you are called to testify—"

My eyes got wide. "Me? Testify?"

He ignored the questions. "Until then . . . *silence.*"

The conversation was very serious, but when I looked at Maude, she was biting her lip to keep from laughing.

It looked like I'd be in the *Tribune* again—and not as a writer. As the butt of another joke, under the headline NEWSGIRL THINKS SHE'S ATTORNEY!

At least the moment gave Miss Giddings a chance to

compose herself. "I don't have anything to say," she told Detective Culhane in a steady voice. "But I suppose this means I won't be released to attend Charles's funeral."

That was the first time I'd thought about Mr. Bessemer getting buried. And though Miss Giddings couldn't go—at least according to Detective Culhane, who didn't seem too sorry to deliver that news—I started to get some very interesting ideas.

Interesting enough that I risked breaking my silence to ask, real nonchalantly, "So, just outta curiosity . . . when is this funeral, anyway?"

CHAPTER 38

LATER THAT DAY, I SAT IN THE ROCKING CHAIR AT ROBERT'S house, trying—and failing—to write a news story about Miss Giddings being innocent. Even though I'd read dozens of articles by Maude and had been sure I could copy her style, nothing I wrote seemed right.

Also, it wasn't easy using paper and a pencil in a chair that kept moving.

I didn't feel like I could get up, though, because Aunt Johnene, who was in the kitchen heating up a can of soup, apparently liked me about as much as Detective Culhane did. Or maybe she just hated everybody. Either way, I got the sense that I should make myself as small and quiet as possible, if I wanted to stay.

Robert was also scared of his aunt and was hunkered down under his blanket, grimacing every time she walked into the room—like she did right then. Carrying, I noticed, only one bowl.

Really?

"Here you go, Robert," she said, setting the soup on the coffee table, a little bit out of easy reach, so he had to scooch around and struggle to get it. It was hard to watch, since he was having one of his bad nights. But his aunt hardly seemed to care that her nephew was fighting for air and his skin was bluish. She glanced at me and finally offered, grudgingly, "Do you want any?"

I knew the right answer to that question, and although my mouth started watering when I caught a whiff of chicken and broth, I said, "No. Thanks, anyhow."

Aunt Johnene—who smelled distinctively *unappetizing*, like mothballs and cabbage—put her hands on her hips, which were quite a bit broader than Miss Giddings's, and peered closely at me. "What did you say you're doing here, again?"

Gosh, in some ways, the two sisters looked alike, but they couldn't have been more different. Miss Giddings was bubbly and sweet, while her sister was just . . . horrible. Aunt Johnene wasn't quite as pretty as Miss Giddings either. Her hair wasn't as shiny, and her mouth didn't have the bowlike quality that made Miss Giddings look like a movie star.

And did I mention the odor that clung to Aunt Johnene?

"Did you say that you and Robert are *friends?*" she asked, so I realized I'd been staring too long and hadn't answered her first question.

"Yeah, we're friends," I confirmed, with a glance at

Robert, who kept his eyes downcast, fixed on his supper. "I'm here so he can help me write a story about Miss . . . about your sister," I added. "To try to get her out of jail."

Johnene Giddings didn't even ask how a story written by a kid might aid in getting an adult out of prison. She rolled her eyes, apparently assuming it was a dumb idea on my part and not worth bothering with. "If you knew anything about Robert's mother, you wouldn't waste your time," she advised me. "Colette created this mess. She needs to get herself out of it. *If* she can."

I reared back in my chair and forgot that I was half afraid of Mean Johnene. "You don't really think your own sister is guilty of murder, do you?"

"I didn't say that," she replied, pursing her lips. That was how she talked, which made her seem snippy and superior. "But I will say that I tried to warn Colette about Charles Bessemer, with his fancy cars and that big diamond he bought her. I knew he was no good, from the moment he tried to approach *me,* at Marshall Field's!"

I looked at Robert again, to see what he thought of his aunt's obvious jealousy, but he still had his nose buried in his bowl, as if he wanted to avoid the whole discussion. He'd probably heard it all before, a thousand times. I was curious, though. "You work at Marshall Field's too?" I asked Aunt Johnene. "Just like Miss Giddings?"

"*Worked,*" she clarified. She puffed out her chest and lifted her chin. "I'm taking a secretarial course now. Making something of myself, unlike every other clerk in

Fine Menswear, who hopes her next husband will walk through the door needing a suit and a bride!"

I admired ladies who made their own way, and I planned to be one of them someday. But I also suspected that given half a chance—unlike Maude Collier, who I honestly believed loved her independence—Johnene Giddings would've been happy to rely on somebody else's cash. In fact, I was pretty sure that she wasn't the one who'd turned down Mr. Bessemer. I had a feeling that once he'd seen Colette Giddings, any flirting he'd done with Johnene had come to a very quick end.

I started to mention that Miss Giddings had a lot of admirers, even in jail, but I knew that would just be rubbing salt in old wounds. Besides, Aunt Johnene wasn't even looking at me. She raised her chin higher and surveyed the cozy little room. "Someday soon I'll have a house just like this one," she muttered. "And I'll pay for it myself!" She seemed to forget that Robert and I—especially Robert—were even there, her gaze continuing to greedily gobble up the furniture. "Maybe even *this* house, if Colette stays in jail and needs to sell it . . ."

"Hey!" I cried, glancing with horror at Robert, who was frozen, wide-eyed, his hand wrapped around his spoon. "Don't say that!" Then I tried to reassure my friend. "You won't lose your house!"

Aunt Johnene seemed to realize she'd gone too far, but she didn't apologize.

"I'm leaving now, Robert," she informed her nephew

as she swept across the room to get her coat. "If you need anything more, please telephone me." She buttoned up, making herself appear even more prim and self-righteous. "But don't abuse the privilege, because the other boarders need the telephone too."

I could just imagine how she lived, crowded into a small place with other single girls who were trying to get by in the city — and living on cheap food, like cabbage. It was a common arrangement, but nowhere near as nice as Miss Giddings having her own snug house — thanks, at least in part, to the prettier sister having snagged *another* man earlier.

All at once I was struck by a thought, and the second the door slammed shut behind Aunt Johnene, I turned to silent Robert, who was clutching his empty bowl.

"Do you think your horrible aunt is jealous and greedy enough to *commit murder?*"

CHAPTER 39

I DON'T KNOW . . ." ROBERT MUSED, SLIDING HIS BOWL ACROSS the coffee table, so that the spoon clattered. He took a labored breath, then managed, "She . . . is bitter . . ."

"Awful!" I agreed. "Nasty and terrible! She practically made you crawl for your dinner." I frowned at what was left of the soup—which was nothing. Not a drop. "And she could've just given me some, without asking. Of course I wanted a bowl!"

Robert's cheeks actually got pinkish. "Sorry. I guess I should've saved you some."

"Yeah. I guess," I agreed. I didn't want to make him feel too bad, though. He'd just been told he might lose his home, and I, of all people, knew what that was like. Our landlady was always knocking on the door, threatening to toss us out. I also knew what it was like to be so hungry that you slurped down whatever was in front of you without even thinking. I changed the subject back to his aunt. "Do you really think she might've been so jealous that she'd take a gun and shoot Mr. Bessemer rather than let your mom marry a rich man?" I hated to bring up a bad subject, but I had to venture, "And maybe frame your mother so she could get this house, too?" My eyes got wide. "Or maybe she meant to kill your mother outright, and she missed in the dark!"

In spite of having watched Butchie McLaughlin and his brothers fight all the time, I could hardly imagine one sibling *killing* another, but Robert seemed to believe my theory was possible. "She always . . . has been very jealous of Mother," he said. "And I'm pretty sure . . . Aunt Johnene liked Mr. Bessemer first." He paused to take a few breaths, and I gave him time. Then he added, "In spite of all the mean comments she . . . she makes about him."

"I suspected that, too," I said. "I could tell the whole thing about wanting to be a secretary and having her own money was just sour grapes."

Robert nodded, and I thought I probably shouldn't push him to keep talking. Before I returned to writing my story, though, I had to ask, "She doesn't chew pepsin gum, does she?"

Aunt Johnene seemed like a person who might have a chronically sour stomach, to match her disposition.

But Robert shook his head. "I don't think so . . ."

He was clearly curious about the question, but I decided not to explain everything I'd found in the alley. He really needed a rest. "You should take a nap now," I suggested. "I'll watch you while I finish my article."

It must've been terrifying to be alone, struggling to breathe, because he didn't seem at all offended by my offer to act as his nanny. He just nodded again, closed his eyes, and tilted his head back, and within a minute his chest was rising and falling in a shallow but steady way.

Poising my pencil over my notebook, I reviewed some of the things I'd written.

New evidence suggests that the woman wrongly accused of being Cook County's "prettiest" killer is actually innocent!! A piece of gum found at the crime scene seems to make it look as if Miss Colette Giddings's mean, almost-former husband could have been there when the fatal shot was fired at mobster Charles Bessemer!

I erased—then added back—the exclamation points about ten times, not sure how Maude managed to make her stories seem so exciting without quite so much punctuation.

What am I doing wrong?

CHAPTER 40

I GOT HOME JUST IN TIME TO SEE MY MOTHER LEAVE FOR HER job. Then I heated up my own can of soup, gulped it down, and climbed into bed. But I couldn't sleep. My article and its shortcomings kept me awake, and before long, I was working on the story again, at the kitchen table.

At dawn, I woke up with my head on the composition book. I still wasn't satisfied with what I'd written, but I dabbed my sleeve on a puddle of drool that had messed up the top page, bundled up, and made my way to the Tribune Tower. Walking straight to an elevator, I asked the operator to take me to the city room, got queasy again, and a few minutes later left three smudged, sometimes torn-by-eraser, and slightly damp pages on Maude's desk.

She wasn't there yet, and I considered taking a few more butterscotches — I was down to two — but the men who were tapping away at typewriters kept sneaking glances at me as if I'd come from Mars. I was pretty sure

I should just leave with empty pockets before somebody dragged me out.

Riding back down, I tugged my cap lower over my ears, ran to the newsstand, picked up my stack of *Tribunes*, and headed for my corner.

Of course I didn't go five steps before I read Maude's byline on the front page, above a story titled PRETTY MURDERESS STILL MARRIED, with a smaller heading, GIDDINGS TO BE TRIED FOR KILLING MOBSTER.

For a second I was really mad. Then I realized that, just like a real reporter, I'd been "scooped." Maude had never promised that she'd wait for me to write a story, and she had probably hurried from the prison to her desk and filed her own.

She treated me just like she would've treated that guy, Tom, from the Herald-Examiner.

Suddenly I was more proud than angry.

I also vowed that, given another chance, I wouldn't get caught napping.

Tucking my papers under my arm, I resumed walking to my spot so I wouldn't miss the crowds of people going to work. But as I looked both ways before crossing the final street, I couldn't help noticing that a certain storefront about half a block away was open for business. A butcher shop, where Albert Rowland—heartless gum chewer who might have killed Charles Bessemer in a jealous rage—supposedly worked.

It couldn't hurt to just take a peek at him, right?

CHAPTER 41

THE THING ABOUT A BUTCHER SHOP IS, PEOPLE DON'T USUally wander in to browse around. They go because they want to buy meat.

Unfortunately, I didn't think of that until I was already inside Swift's Meats, a bell on the door jangling as it closed behind me, which alerted the man behind the counter to my presence, so he turned around.

The first thing I noticed was the scowl on his face.

Then the big bloodstains on his white apron.

Then the name that was stitched on that apron so customers would know who was handing them their roasts and chops.

Albert!

CHAPTER 42

"WHADDYA WANT, KID?"

Robert's dad set down a huge cleaver, wiped his hands on his apron, adding to the bloodstains, and came over to the big glass counter, which was filled with red meat in various shapes and sizes. Part of me was disgusted by the sight, and especially by the nearly overpowering smell of blood and raw flesh. But to be honest, part of me wished I could buy a steak.

Which, of course, I couldn't do. I didn't have any money at all. My unsold papers were waiting in a stack just outside the door.

So why was I there? What had I hoped to accomplish?

"Hurry it up, kid," Mr. Rowland grumbled. By most standards, he was a very handsome man, with dark, slicked-back hair and a narrow, fashionable mustache. But he was also ugly in a way that I couldn't quite put my finger on. He wasn't just stiff-necked, like Detective Culhane. No, Robert's dad seemed *mean*. And it wasn't only the stained clothes that made him unpleasant. It was the grim set of his mouth and the impatient way he glowered at me and . . . well, the fact that he'd walked out on his family. Knowing that probably made a big difference in how I viewed Albert Rowland.

He *shoulda married Aunt Johnene!*

"I got a half steer to butcher," he advised me. "You want somethin' or not?"

"I . . . I was just . . ."

I started to ask for some kind of meat—the word *T-bone* came to mind—thinking I would run away when he turned around to wrap it up.

Then I really looked into Mr. Rowland's eyes, which were hard and cold, and I thought about Miss Giddings, who had obviously made a bad choice but was trying to get unstuck from it, and about Robert, too.

My *friend*, Robert, who maybe did let his polio get him down, but likely didn't believe in himself because his own father had called him a weakling and been too ashamed to even raise him.

I thought of all those things—except about how Albert Rowland had possibly *killed a man*, because if I'd remembered that, I probably wouldn't have blurted out, "I'm here because I had to see the terrible person who abandoned my best friend, Robert Giddings, just because he got a disease. And I want to tell you that I think you are just *awful*."

As I said all that, I realized that Robert really was my

best friend. It also hit me that I should've made sure I had the right Albert before scolding him. So as I marched to the door, leaving a very stunned and red-with-rage butcher thankfully trapped behind his counter, I quickly turned back. "You *are* Albert *Rowland,* right?"

He didn't answer, but I could tell from his expression that I'd been correct.

"Oh, and by the way," I added, one hand on the door, ready to push it open. "I think you might've killed Charles Bessemer and are letting a very nice lady sit in prison for *your* crime!"

I could hardly believe those words had tumbled out of my mouth, and I tore outside, my dramatic exit diminished by the cheerful tinkling of the shop bell.

Only when I was safe, a block away, having scooped up my papers and run as fast as I could, did I take a deep breath and wonder, *What have I just done?*

CHAPTER 43

I WAS IN MY BEDROOM THE NEXT DAY TRYING TO FIND SOME-
thing suitable to wear to a funeral, given that I mainly
owned cast-off boys' pants—who could sell newspapers
in a *dress?*—when all of a sudden I heard a knock at the
front door.

Tossing aside a pair of old knickers that didn't even fit
anymore, I grabbed Dad's flannel bathrobe, my absolute
favorite memento of him. I never let it get washed, although Mom said it was probably time.

As I fumbled to tie the robe around me, the visitor
rapped on the door again, and I ran through the house
before that could happen a third time. The last thing I
needed was my mother waking up and asking me about
my plans for the day. How would I explain that I needed
to attend a mobster's burial?

"We'll have the rent Friday, Mrs. Leeds!" I promised
before I even twisted the knob. "Just . . ."

But when I peeked outside, I saw that Mom and I weren't in trouble for getting behind on the rent.

Well, we were probably in trouble, but it wasn't Mrs. Leeds on our porch. Yet.

Nope. I was getting a surprise visit from somebody who for once wanted to *help* me.

CHAPTER 44

"YOU'RE SURE IT DOESN'T COST EXTRA TO TAKE ME?" I ASKED Maude, who didn't seem excited at all to be riding in a Checker Cab, no doubt because she did it all the time. For me, the whole thing was a novelty, and I wasn't even positive how you paid for it. I was more familiar with *not* paying for streetcar rides. "If I'm costing you money," I added, "I could give you some."

Maude had obviously heard me trying to put off paying the rent, but just like in the diner, she pretended I was well-off. "Of course you could pay your way," she said. "But honestly, it doesn't matter how many people take the ride."

"Well, thanks for coming to get me," I said, settling back in the seat. I wished the funeral was farther away, because the cab was pretty nice. "I was sure surprised to see you."

"You're certain that your mother is all right with this?" she asked. "Shouldn't you have asked permission . . ."

"I'm not supposed to wake her up," I explained. "And she knows I can take care of myself."

"Okay."

Maude spoke softly, and I saw concern in her eyes. The kind of pity I didn't want from her, any more than I wanted charity. "I really can watch out for myself," I promised. "I can!"

Maude smiled. "Yes, I know that."

Craning my neck, I tried to see the road ahead. "How did you even know I wanted to go?"

"I could tell—by the way you pretended *not* to care when the funeral was—that you'd attend. And I would've done the same thing in your place. You don't want to miss this if you're covering—or solving—the murder."

I twisted in my seat, getting excited. "Yes! That's exactly what I thought! Everybody who knew Mr. Bessemer will be there." Then I remembered the article I'd given Maude, and I simmered down a little. "I guess I'm not much of a reporter, though. You haven't even mentioned my story—which was a big mess, I know."

"Oh, goodness, Isabel!" Maude dug into her purse until she located three sheets of lined paper, one of which had a stain from being drooled on. "I forgot I had this!" She handed me the article. "I hope you don't mind, but I made some suggestions."

Accepting the folded papers, I opened them. There was ink everywhere. "Yeah, you sure did!"

Maude laughed. "You should've seen *my* first stories

after my editor was finished with them. And I'd been to college!" She nudged me. "I think you did quite well, Izzie. Very promising!"

I watched to see if she was just saying stuff, like adults often did. "Honest?"

"Honest."

I could tell she meant it.

"Do you *really* think Albert Rowland might be the killer?" she asked. "Just because he chews a certain type of gum?"

"Enough that I sort of accidentally accused him of the murder," I confided, trying to make myself smaller. I was sure by then that I'd made a terrible mistake back in the butcher shop.

Maude laughed out loud. "You did *what?*"

"I stopped by Swift's Meats—just to see him," I explained. "And he was so mean, trying to force me to buy meat—"

"It *is* a butcher shop," Maude noted, still grinning.

I ignored the teasing. "I ended up telling him that he was a terrible father and probably murdered Charles Bessemer too."

Maude got more serious. "Goodness, Isabel . . . I don't think that was a very good idea. What if you've angered him?"

I recalled Albert Rowland's bright red face. "Oh, I'm sure I did that." Sitting up straighter, I studied Maude. "But if Miss Giddings is the killer and Mr. Rowland is innocent—like you believe—then why would he care if some kid accuses him of murder?"

Maude opened her mouth to speak, then shut it. I'd obviously stumped her. Still, she wasn't going to admit that maybe, just maybe, Miss Giddings was innocent. "I suppose you have a point," she finally said. She shot me a warning look. "Don't go around accusing anyone else, though, all right?" She gestured at the story I was still clutching. "Especially in print."

"But you do it—"

"Based upon years of experience, Isabel." She cut me off before I could remind her that she was always convicting killers in the *Tribune.* "Before you start printing accusations, wait until you've been a reporter for as long as I have."

I liked that she was talking as if being a reporter was my destiny. As if there was no way it wouldn't happen. Smiling, I tucked the story into my coat so I could study her notes later. Then I switched pockets because the right-hand lining had just torn, costing me my last two butterscotches.

"Are you sure I look okay?" I asked for probably the tenth time. I'd ended up wearing the same clothes I wore to sell newspapers: my hand-me-down pants, my dad's old cap, and my shabby coat. "I don't wanna stand out." I pictured Flora Bessemer, who'd probably wear that beret. "Flora's probably gonna have on velvet and jewels."

Maude gave me a curious look. "How do you know about her?"

"I met her once," I said. "She came to the alley when I was snooping around, and she practically decked me!"

"So you're acquainted with both Albert Rowland *and* Flora?" Clearly impressed, Maude bent to look at me better. "Because I have been trying to speak with Flora about her father—and Miss Giddings—but her uncle is very determined to keep her away from the press."

"Yeah, he was at the alley too. He's scary."

Maude stared straight ahead again, biting her nail, which was painted dark red. "Interesting . . ."

"You know, I also know Miss Giddings's sister," I told Maude. "Have you talked with her yet?"

"I've tried," Maude admitted. "But with little success."

"Well, Robert's aunt is real jealous of Miss Giddings," I informed her. "Aunt Johnene liked Mr. Bessemer first, but he went for the prettier sister. Now she's trying to be a secretary—and get Miss Giddings's house, cheap."

Maude eyed me warily. "You didn't accuse *her,* too . . ."

"No. Not yet."

"Izzie!" Maude started to scold me, then realized I was joking. Or sort of joking. "I'll give you credit," she said. "You are taking this investigation seriously."

"So will you tell Detective Culhane? About Aunt Johnene? And Albert Rowland? And explain the things I found in the alley?"

"I'll consider it," Maude said. She nudged me with her

elbow. "Thanks for the information about Johnene Giddings."

"Yeah, no problem." I knew Maude well enough by then not to pressure her to talk with Detective Culhane. She'd think over what I'd told her and do what she wanted. And I was getting distracted, worrying about my clothes again. "You're *sure* I look okay?"

Maude gave my arm a reassuring pat. "Trust me, Isabel—you will *not* stand out." The taxicab slowed, and she searched in her purse again, this time for money. "No one will even notice you."

I thought that was strange, because from what I understood, funerals were very private and formal. But when Maude had thanked the driver and helped me out the door and I got a good look into Mount Carmel Cemetery, I realized she was right.

Nobody was gonna care that I was there.

Heck, I just hoped we could get close to the service. For a man who'd been murdered, Charles Bessemer really seemed to have a lot of friends.

My stomach suddenly got tickly with excitement.

And maybe —just maybe—at least one enemy might be in that huge crowd too. A "mourner" who was only pretending to grieve, to cover up the fact that he or she had *killed* Mr. Bessemer.

CHAPTER 45

P EOPLE IN CHICAGO LOVE A GOOD MOB FUNERAL," MAUDE whispered while a minister went on and on about eternity. I was starting to get a pretty good sense of what forever felt like, standing graveside. Just as we got jostled —again—Maude added, "There's always a crowd."

That was an understatement. The cemetery was packed, and I was squished between Maude and the reporter named Tom, who'd wanted the telephone back at the police station.

Why was everybody so interested in men who sold booze and killed each other?

And why did mobsters want reporters to cover their funerals? Once Maude had pushed her way close to the grave, we'd been pulled even closer by two very large men in very dark suits who led us to a special area where a whole bunch of people had notebooks.

I craned my neck—not to see the casket, which was

silver, as if Mr. Bessemer were stuffed in a big bullet getting shot to heaven. Or to the other place.

No, I was looking at one of the men who'd ushered me and Maude to our spot.

Flora Bessemer's uncle.

Up close, he loomed even bigger and was shaped like a barrel that had a head balanced on top. Honestly, he had no neck to speak of. And his face was like a bulldog's, the features all pushed in.

I peered closer.

And was he *eating* something during the service? I could see his big jowls flapping.

I didn't know much about funerals, but I was pretty sure you shouldn't bring a snack. It just seemed disrespectful.

I guess I wasn't very respectful either when I tugged Maude's sleeve and whispered, "Get a load of the guy chowing down!"

She started to grin—then abruptly got serious and returned her attention to her notebook, her pencil poised. I stood on tiptoes to see the front-row mourners again and perked up my ears, trying to figure out what had captured her interest.

And lo and behold, I got pretty intrigued too, because none other than *Flora Bessemer* was stepping up near the minister, preparing herself to say a few words about her father.

CHAPTER 46

THE FLORA BESSEMER I SAW AT THE CEMETERY WAS NOTH-ing like the one I'd met in the alley.

No, the girl in the black wool coat who stood framed by a huge horseshoe of roses was almost cloyingly cute. She didn't vow revenge for her father's death. She just talked about how sweet "dear Papa" had been. The ice in those blue eyes had melted into tears too—although I thought they seemed a little forced.

Back in the alley, I'd seen Flora get genuinely sad, if only for a moment, but this was different. And if I hadn't met her before and listened as she coolly promised to settle a score, I probably would've bought the whole act.

"Oh, Papa!" she cried, her eyes toward heaven, although the more I thought about it, I was pretty sure that really was the wrong direction to be looking. The crowd lapped it up, though. A bunch of old ladies started sobbing when Flora sniffed, "How I shall miss your tender, generous heart!"

Don't get me wrong. I believed Flora loved and would miss her dad.

But she wasn't a weeper.

And as for her father having a "tender" heart . . . well, anybody who palled around with Al Capone wasn't exactly a big softie.

Heck, there were *guns* at the funeral. I'd seen one, only half hidden under Flora's uncle's coat.

My eyes must've gotten wide because when he walked away, Maude whispered, "There are lots of firearms here. No respectable mobster would be caught in a crowd like this without one!"

But to hear Flora talk, her dad had been a saint.

"Father always took care of our neighbors . . ." She droned on, almost as bad as the minister. "Even when we had very little, before I became famous . . ."

She had to put *that* in there. Like being in a bread advertisement was all that great!

". . . Papa would share what we had with those around us . . ."

I tugged Maude's sleeve. "Flora's layin' it on a little thick, huh?"

Maude leaned close, laughing. "Now who's being cynical?"

She was teasing me because I believed Miss Giddings was innocent but thought Flora was full of baloney when it came to "Papa's" virtues. "This is different," I said. "Everybody knows mobsters are bad."

"Yet this city loves them," Maude said softly, poising her pencil over her notebook again. She shook her head. "It's a mystery."

"Sure is. Why make such a fuss over men who break the law then end up killing each other?"

I might've said that a little too loud. All at once, Mount Carmel Cemetery got very quiet, and some people turned to look at me. Including, unfortunately, Flora Bessemer, who wasn't crying anymore.

Nope.

Those blue eyes were deadly *ice* again.

CHAPTER 47

THAT WAS QUITE A SCENE WE CAUSED," MAUDE NOTED, keeping one gloved hand on my shoulder so we wouldn't get separated as we exited the graveyard. Even more people had shown up while we'd been listening to Flora's big eulogy. And Mr. Bessemer wasn't even a big-time mobster. If he hadn't gotten shot, nobody would've known who he was.

What a crazy city. No wonder the whole rest of the country thought Chicago was loony for guns and gangsters. I guess we were.

"Flora looked like she was going to kill me," I said without exaggerating. I searched for little Miss Bessemer in the crowd. The barrel of a man was helping her into a long, dark automobile.

But right before she climbed into the seat, Flora spotted me too—and stopped dead in her tracks.

CHAPTER 48

"WOULD YOU MIND IF I SPOKE TO HER IN PRIVATE, PLEASE?" Flora asked Maude, pointing to me. She was being overly polite in that way adults always like. "It will just take a moment."

"There's quite a crowd," Maude noted, glancing around. "I'd like to stay close to Izzie."

I knew Maude wasn't really worried about me getting lost in a cemetery or stolen away by strangers in broad daylight. I sold papers alone on a street corner, for crying out loud.

She was just being a nosy reporter, trying to finagle that interview she wanted with Flora. However, before I could say it was fine with me if Maude listened, Flora's uncle stuck his bulldog nose into the conversation.

"They can talk in the car," he offered—not in a friendly way. In a *Butt out, lady* way. "They'll be fine."

"I don't know about *that*." Maude frowned with more genuine concern at the prospect of me actually getting into a mobster's automobile. "I feel responsible for Isabel today, and she doesn't really know you . . ."

I was positive that Maude would've leaped into that long, black sedan, though, if it meant she could get an interview. Reporters did things like that, right?

"I'll be okay," I assured her, trying to give her a look that said, *I'll ask questions. Tell you what she says!*

Maude hesitated, then turned to the big uncle. "All right. Just for a moment, though."

Then she gave me a look. One that said, *Be careful— but get news.*

All at once I realized that we were kind of *working together.* And although I was excited, I wanted to act very professional. "I'll be right back," I promised, as if I helped out famous journalists every day. Then I followed Flora into the biggest auto I'd ever been in—and lost a little of my nerve when the uncle slammed the door on both of us.

Flora, meanwhile, lost her charm.

The second we were alone, she started to interview *me,* dropping the polite, sweet voice and demanding, "What are *you* doing here, *alley cat?*"

CHAPTER 49

WHY'D YOU CALL ME THAT?" I ASKED, MY CHEEKS FLUSH-ing with indignation.

"I found you crawling around garbage cans," Flora reminded me. She looked me up and down, and I knew Maude hadn't been completely right about my outfit. At least one person had noticed that I wasn't exactly dressed for a funeral. "What are you doing here now?"

"I'm trying to find out what really happened to your dad," I told her. It was hard to concentrate, though, because I felt like *I* was in a coffin. The sedan was huge, but somehow cramped and suffocating. Maybe it was the way the door had thunked shut behind me, or the fact that I couldn't hear anything outside. "Jeez," I added, tugging at my collar, "is there enough air in here?"

"The car is bulletproof and sealed tight," Flora explained impatiently. "You get used to it."

So she obviously knew her father's real business. "What do you want with me?" I asked, suddenly afraid that I was going to get "taken for a ride." And not a nice Sunday drive either. No, the kind mobsters gave each other. Meaning somebody ended up dead. "Why'd you wanna talk to me?"

"First I find you snooping around where my father got *killed*," Flora said, watching me with her shrewd eyes. "Then you show up at his funeral with a reporter. Seems kind of funny to me."

Obviously not "ha-ha" funny.

"So you know who Maude is?" I asked, thinking maybe Flora and I had something in common. Newspapers. "Do you read the *Tribune*?"

But she looked at me like I was stupid. "I don't read the newspapers. I am *in* the newspapers. And Maude Collier has been trying to talk to me for days."

"Oh, right." Here I was, with a chance to get information out of Flora Bessemer, and the first questions I asked were the dumbest ones possible. And my next question probably wasn't much better. "Why don't you wanna be interviewed?"

"Uncle Carl doesn't think it would be in my best interest," Flora said. "If a reporter *misunderstood* something I said and it got into the papers, it could ruin my movie contract."

I hated the snooty way she said that, with a flip of her curls, but my eyes got wide anyhow. "You're gonna be in a *movie*?"

She had already given up caring about *me* now that

the topic was *her.* "Yes," she informed me. "A real Hollywood movie! With Marion Davies!"

Okay, that was impressive. Marion Davies was famous, right up there with Clara Bow and Mary Pickford. "How'd you go from selling bread to being in a movie?" I asked. "That's a pretty big jump!"

"Uncle Carl knows people with the studios," she said. "So did my father. They got me a screen test when we visited California last year." She glanced at my clothes again. "You wouldn't understand."

All of a sudden I forgot that Uncle Carl probably also had connections that could get me *killed,* and I warned her, "I ought to pop you one! Why are you so mean?"

Flora didn't answer. "Why, really, are you poking your nose into my father's murder?" she asked again. "Tell the truth!"

"I just want to help Miss Giddings," I said. "And her son, Robert. Because Miss Giddings is going on trial, and Robert is—"

"I know all about Robert Giddings," Flora interrupted. "His mother was worried about taking him to California, if that's where we had to move for my career." Flora rolled her soon-to-be-even-more-famous eyes. "She doesn't like to 'disrupt' him."

"I was just going to say that he's my *friend,*" I told her. "I want to help Miss Giddings and Robert because we're *friends.*"

Flora Bessemer might've had a "career," but I was

pretty sure she didn't have any more friends than I did. Maybe fewer. I also got the feeling she didn't care.

"Who do you really think killed your father?" I asked, cutting to the chase. "And let's not pretend that everything you said a few minutes ago, about him being a saint, was true."

I thought Flora might pop *me* for saying that. "Don't you ever say anything bad about my father," she growled. "You didn't know him!"

The tears at the funeral had definitely been a bit much, but once again, I saw a flash of genuine grief, expressed as anger. "Sorry," I said. "I shouldn't have said that."

I didn't think she'd forgive me, but she muttered, "It's okay." Then she paused, and I got the feeling that as hard and cold as she was, she wished she had somebody to confide in. "I'm not sure who killed him," she said. "But I have suspicions . . ."

I was about to burst with excitement, and I held my breath, afraid that if I even sucked in some air, she'd stop talking.

Unfortunately, at that very moment Uncle Carl opened the door and poked his head in. "Flora? We need to get going."

His breath stank up the already close air, and I fought the urge to wave my hand in front of my nose.

What had he been snacking on during the funeral? Garlic cloves and . . . what was that other smell?

"Just give us one more minute," Flora snapped. It was

clear that, though she was only a kid, she was in charge, just like Detective Culhane bossed around the older Hastings. "Shut the door!"

Uncle Carl did as he was told, and Flora returned her attention to me.

"Look," I said. "You and I have different reasons for wanting to solve this crime. Me, to save somebody. And you, so you can kill somebody."

Flora didn't object to that. In fact, it seemed to strike her as quite reasonable. So I kept talking. "Why don't we team up? Because—even though I think you're snooty and mean—you're obviously very smart. And I am too."

Flora blinked at me about ten times, and I thought she was going to say I was crazy.

But I guess being direct worked with her. "Fine," she agreed. "What do we do next?"

It struck me then that maybe she'd wanted a partner all along.

As I left that sedan after making plans to meet her again, I also realized that I'd just formed an alliance with a mobster's daughter to track down a killer who might turn out to be an honest-to-gosh *hit man*. And between Flora and me, only one of us got to travel in the safety of a bulletproof auto.

Worse yet, when I opened the door of that car, who was waiting for me, standing next to Maude?

Why, Detective James Culhane, of course!

CHAPTER 50

"I SUPPOSE I SHOULD HAVE EXPECTED THAT YOU WOULD SHOW up at the funeral, Miss Feeney," Detective Culhane said without taking his eyes off the traffic. I was riding in his official police car again, stuck in the back seat this time because Maude was up front. He frowned at her. "However, I am a little surprised that you two seem to be collaborating."

By "surprised," he obviously meant "disappointed" and "disapproving."

"Isabel is quite insightful and helpful," Maude said, turning to smile and wink at me, as though she found his grumpiness amusing and wanted me in on the joke. She turned back around. "I've been trying to get an interview with Flora Bessemer for days, with no result, and Izzie got invited right into Flora's private auto."

"I didn't learn that much," I pointed out. That wasn't entirely my fault, so I added, "Just as she was about to name a bunch of people who might've killed her dad, *Uncle Carl* had to stick his big nose into the conversation and ruin everything."

Detective Culhane gave me a quick, intrigued look. "Is that true? She has suspicions?"

It was the first time he seemed interested in pinning the crime on anybody but Miss Giddings, and I got so excited that I jumped forward, so *my* nose was in between him and Maude. Of course, he immediately advised me, "Sit back, please, Isabel."

"Okay, fine." I did as I was told, but at least I didn't have to button my lip. "Flora doesn't think Miss Giddings killed her dad," I informed him. "She thinks Miss Giddings is innocent!"

That was a bit of a stretch. Flora hadn't *exactly* said that. But given how she loved revenge, if she believed, for one second, that Miss Giddings really was guilty, she'd probably go to the Cook County Jail in person and make good on that vow she'd made in the alley.

Maude shifted in her seat—*she* was allowed to move around—so she could see me again. "What else did you and Flora speak about, Izzie? You were in there quite a while."

I almost confided that Flora and I had formed a partnership, but something—or, more accurately, someone—made me keep that to myself. A certain detective who had gotten quiet but was no doubt listening carefully and watching me with those eyes he had in the back of his head. The ones that had caught Hastings napping. "Aw, she was mostly bragging about how she's gonna be in a big movie with Marion Davies," I finally said. "She's all full of herself about how her family 'knows' people in Hollywood."

I thought the stuff about the movie wasn't very important. In fact, that was why I said it. So I was surprised when Detective Culhane glanced sharply at Maude, while she smiled in a knowing way and arched her perfect eyebrows. "Interesting," Maude said, as if she'd just learned something big. "Very interesting!"

What . . .

I poked my nose up front again, looking from one to the other. "What'd I say?"

They ignored me. Detective Culhane didn't even tell me to butt out. He spoke quietly to Maude, as if he'd forgotten I existed. "All these thugs have connections to the movie studios. Booze and entertainment . . . it's all intertwined."

To my disappointment, Maude seemed to have forgotten me too. "A very pretty young department store clerk might have desperately wanted those connections," she mused aloud. "What an easy way to fame and fortune!"

I finally understood that they were talking about Miss Giddings, and how she might've been using Charles Bessemer to get a career in the movies. I'd always thought she was pretty enough . . .

"Miss Giddings wouldn't do that!" I cried. "She only wanted his *money*—for Robert! To cure him!"

As soon as the words were out of my mouth, I knew I'd made a big mistake. It was too late to fix it, though. Maude and Detective Culhane had just heard me admit that Miss Giddings had wanted her dead boyfriend's money. They probably hadn't even noticed the part about Robert.

I thudded back in my seat. "Why would she kill him if she wanted fame—or his money, even?" I asked glumly. "Didn't she need him alive to get that stuff?"

"Oh, Isabel . . ." Maude said. "These complicated affairs don't always end logically. Maybe Bessemer told your Miss Giddings that he couldn't get her into the movies. Maybe he was cutting the money off. You don't know what they were arguing about the night he was shot."

"Miss Giddings didn't want to move to Hollywood," I told Maude, crossing my arms over my chest. "She didn't want to 'disrupt' Robert. That's the exact word Flora used. *Disrupt.*"

Maude and Detective Culhane shared another look, only this time they weren't smirking. "That is surprising," Maude conceded.

"Yes, it is," Detective Culhane agreed.

Had I actually convinced them, a little, to at least consider Miss Giddings as possibly innocent?

It seemed that way. And I suddenly realized that De-

tective Culhane's attendance at the funeral was probably
a good sign, too. He must've gone because he was still
investigating, right?

"You really should tell him about Albert Rowland and
Aunt Johnene," I urged Maude. "About the things I told
you—"

"What things?" Detective Culhane interrupted.

Maude gave me another quick smile. Then she told
Detective Culhane, "Isabel has done some investigating, and she considers both Robert's aunt and Albert
Rowland potential suspects. She's gone so far as to
visit Mr. Rowland's butcher shop and accuse him of
the murder—"

Detective Culhane stomped on the brake, although
we weren't at a place a car should normally stop, and
ignoring a honking horn behind us, he turned to Maude.
"She did what?"

"I'll tell you everything later, James," she promised.
"There's no harm done." Maude waggled her fingers,
urging him to keep driving. "Go on, now."

He accelerated again, then addressed me in a low,
measured tone. "Did we not agree that you would *keep
your nose out of this case*, Miss Feeney?"

"Not exactly . . . It was more like you *telling* me . . .
But I didn't *agree* . . ."

Maude was shaking her head, just slightly, silently
urging me to shut up. I took the advice and let her de-

fend me. "Isabel has quite a few compelling theories, James. I'm not sure I agree with her conclusions, or her methods, but she did unearth possible motives for both Johnene Giddings and Albert Rowland."

Detective Culhane wasn't convinced. "I can't believe I'm even listening to secondhand gossip from a murdered man's kid, let alone the investigative 'findings' of another child," he grumbled.

"Hey!" I was supposed to keep quiet, but that comment really irritated me. "Why do you always think kids are stupid?"

I seemed to have caught him off-guard. He gave me an uncertain glance over his shoulder. "I never said that."

"Yeah, you just did!" I protested. "And you didn't even think I could spell *gun,* remember?"

For the first time since I'd met him, Detective Culhane kind of *blushed.* Probably because I was making him look like a kid-hating meanie in front of Maude. "I . . . I didn't mean any insult," he stammered. He looked at Maude. "I really didn't . . ."

She was laughing. "You can be harsh with children, James."

"And with poor Hastings," I added while I had the chance. "He's scared to death of you!"

I'd obviously pushed things too far, because he got very quiet again. He didn't even talk to Maude. But I saw her move, and though my view of her hand was blocked by the seat, I was pretty sure she nudged him, wordlessly telling him not to be so serious.

He glanced at her, as if he got the message, and something about those little gestures made me really sorry for both of them. They belonged together. So why not . . .

It struck me that they were probably right about adults' relationships being difficult for kids—even smart ones—to fully understand.

"This is your house, correct, Isabel?" Detective Culhane asked, breaking what was becoming a long silence.

I hadn't even realized we'd reached my street. I'd been too busy watching him and Maude to look out the window. But when I did, sure enough, I was home. "Thanks for the ride," I said, opening the door and getting out. Then I poked my head back in. "Sorry I got mad at you, Detective Culhane."

He twisted to look at me, and to my complete shock said, "I'm sorry too, Isabel. I didn't mean to imply that you—or children in general—are stupid."

"I will go to school again, someday, and be somebody," I informed him. "I will!"

I had no idea why I said that. It was a terrible mistake.

"You don't *ever* go to school?" he asked.

The last thing I needed was more attention from truant officers. Fortunately, they were busy chasing lots of kids and had so far only left notes at our house, saying they'd like to talk with my mom.

"Aw, I go sometimes," I said, crossing my fingers behind my back.

Detective Culhane didn't seem like he was going to make trouble for me, though. He almost looked sad.

"Just do your best to attend, okay?" he suggested.

"Okay," I agreed.

We stared at each other for a long moment. As I moved to shut the door, I heard Maude calling after me, "Don't forget to read my notes on your story!"

I *had* forgotten my article, but when she reminded me, I hurried inside, hopped onto my bed, pulled the folded papers out of my pocket, and started to read with a half-excited, half-sick feeling in the pit of my stomach.

"Dear, dear Isabel . . ."

CHAPTER 51

MAUDE'S HANDWRITING WAS TERRIBLE, PROBABLY BE-cause she was used to taking notes on her little pad, writing too quickly to be neat, but I could tell that she'd taken time to read my mess of a story carefully.

Each paragraph was marked up, enough that I got pretty discouraged by the third sentence. Apparently I did use way too many exclamation points, and even I had to admit that I'd gotten sloppy with my spelling toward the end.

But just when I thought my dreams of being a reporter were crushed, I read the note she'd scrawled on the back of one of the sheets. A little message I'd seen when I'd unfolded the papers, but had saved for last.

Dear, dear Isabel . . .

Nobody'd ever called me a double "dear" before, and I almost wanted to stop right there, before I got to the inevitable bad parts. But of course, I had to read the whole thing.

> *I realize that I've turned a very critical eye on your story. However, that's only because I believe strongly in your potential. You have all the attributes of a good reporter—curiosity, determination to seek the truth, and courage—as well as the uncanny ability to show up at the right—or wrong?—place at the right—or wrong!—time.*

I guess it was okay for *her* to use exclamation points.

> *Most important, you have a good heart. Perhaps that's something journalism needs in this modern, jaded age, and especially in this violent city, where murder has become so commonplace that we often joke about it.*

I took a second to think about that. Was I living in a "jaded" age? I had no idea, because it was all I'd ever known. I knew that I lived in a violent city, though. But had there really been a time when people in Chicago . . .

All at once I thought about the Great War, which had claimed millions of lives and pretty much ruined mine, and I corrected myself.

Had there been a time when people all over the *world* didn't kill each other without hardly a second thought?

I wasn't sure, so I kept reading.

One word of advice: When you write your next story—
and I do hope you write many more—ignore what you
see in the Tribune every day, including my own work.
    Next time, write an ISABEL story.
    THAT—more than correct spelling or punctuation
—will be the key to your success as a journalist.

I set down the note, confused and discouraged, in spite of her kind words.

Wasn't I supposed to write like every other reporter? Wasn't that the whole idea?

And why wouldn't Maude want me to copy her, like I *had* tried to do, since she was the best journalist in town?

Turning over the paper, I looked at my marked-up writing again, even more baffled and worried about my chances of ever being a real reporter.

Because what the heck would an "ISABEL" story even be?

CHAPTER 52

I CAN'T BELIEVE SHE'S REALLY COMING HERE," ROBERT COM-
plained, using his blanket to wipe his fingers clean of
Vicks VapoRub. I'd brought the blue jar from my mother's medicine cabinet and given him a big glob to smear
on his chest. Mom swore the pungent goo made breathing easier, and maybe she was right. Robert already
seemed a little better—except for his mood, which had
been terrible ever since I'd told him that Flora Bessemer
was stopping by. "I thought I was free of her—"

All at once, Robert's eyes got wide, and he stopped
himself.

At first I didn't understand why. Then I realized that
he'd just admitted that, though Charles Bessemer's murder had messed up his life in one way, putting his mother
in jail, something good had come of it too. And knowing Flora the way I did now, I could imagine how badly
somebody would want her to go away.

I'd been about to offer Robert part of a sandwich I'd

brought from home—because *I* shared—then I stopped and studied the boy I considered a friend but still didn't know that well.

But Robert would never . . . could never . . . no matter how desperate he'd gotten . . .

"What's wrong?" he asked, furrowing his brow. "Why are you staring at me funny?"

"No reason," I said, tearing apart the sandwich. Wonder Bread with peanut butter. It wasn't much to split, but I hadn't felt like I could make extras, since I hadn't been selling a lot of papers lately and had swiped my mother's medicine, too. Maybe VapoRub was expensive. I handed Robert his share. "Eat up."

Robert took a bite—then nearly choked when the door opened wide, without anybody even knocking, and in walked little Miss Flora Bessemer, making a grand entrance, as if she were the star of *this* production, too.

Needless to say, her bodyguard wasn't far behind.

CHAPTER 53

HOW'D YOU GET TO BE IN CHARGE OF SOMEBODY SO BIG AND scary?" I asked Flora after she'd dismissed Uncle Carl to wait in the car. "Adults never listen to *me*."

"You don't have a movie contract," she sniffed.

"What's that have to do with it?" Robert piped up. He'd been pretty quiet since their awkward reunion. Flora had greeted him with a complaint about the stink of the VapoRub, and Robert's condolences hadn't rung too sincere either. They really would've made terrible siblings. "It's just a stupid movie," he added. "It doesn't make you anybody's boss."

"It's worth a lot of money," Flora pointed out, making herself at home on one of the high-backed chairs. I took my place on the rocker. "And as my new legal guardian, Uncle Carl could be *rich,* if I get more roles— which will probably happen." When we didn't ask why she was so confident, Flora took it upon herself to brag.

"My screen test went *very* well." She smiled smugly. "Uncle Carl knows he should keep me happy."

"Or what?" I asked. "If he's your guardian . . ."

The smile got even more smug. "I could petition the court for another guardian if he was ever cruel to me."

"Flora!" I cried. "You're practically blackmailing your own uncle into being your slave!"

She rolled her eyes. "He wants the money. He doesn't *have* to do anything."

Robert and I shared a look, both of us clearly thinking, *That's a very interesting way to look at family!*

Then, although we were there to solve a crime, I couldn't help asking, "What happened to your mom, Flora? Did she die or something?"

Flora got that icy look in her eyes. The expression that I was starting to learn sometimes masked hurt. "I don't know where she is. And I don't care. She left me when I wasn't even a year old and never wrote a letter or anything. Not even on my birthday."

Robert and I looked at each other again, and frowned. He also obviously understood that she really did care.

"Sorry," he and I said in unison. I knew that he, especially, could sympathize with Flora.

"I guess we all have something in common," I told them both. "Something *awful*."

For the first time, Flora looked at me as if I might be remotely interesting. "How so?"

"My dad got killed in the war. I've only got a mom."

The hard glint in Flora's eyes softened. "Sorry."

I believed she meant it.

"Yeah, well, we aren't here to cry about the past, are we?" I reminded them, picking up my composition book, which I'd set on the coffee table. "We're here to help Robert's mom." Because I knew that wasn't Flora's main goal, I added, "And to . . . er, 'avenge' your dad, right?"

She pursed her lips and nodded.

"So," I said, licking the tip of my pencil and getting ready to write, "let's start with that list of suspects you mentioned at the funeral, huh, Flora?"

CHAPTER 54

I T WAS A GOOD THING I LICKED THAT PENCIL TO GET THE LEAD started, because Flora had a huge list of people who'd hated her dad. And most of them had names like Johnny Two Guns and Mike the Nose.

"Why 'the Nose'?" I asked when she took a breath.

"It got shot off," she informed me, like that happened to people every day.

Robert was shaking his head, as if he couldn't believe he'd almost become part of the Bessemer family. And for the first time, my faith in Miss Giddings was a little rattled. I still didn't believe she'd kill anybody, but I had to ask, "Robert . . . could your mom really not have known she was seeing a mobster?" I gave Flora a guilty glance. "Sorry."

She shrugged. "That's what he was."

I turned back to Robert. "Really? She knew nothing?"

He hesitated, like he was uncertain, and Flora answered for him. "Oh, it's possible." She puffed up with what I thought was misplaced pride. "My father wasn't one of those gangsters like Al Capone or Dean O'Banion, who have to be all showy. Lots of people, even folks close to him, thought he was strictly a legitimate auto sales-man. Daddy always said it's the flashy guys who end up dead."

"And yet . . ." Robert started to question that logic, but I shook my head, and he stopped himself.

Meanwhile, I was still confused about Miss Giddings. "But Flora . . . didn't your dad carry a gun, at least?"

Flora just laughed. "Who *doesn't* carry a gun in Chi-cago?"

She had a point.

"So what do we do next?" Robert asked. "We have a bunch of names, but what can we do with them?"

I had an idea. "We should go to the police station to-morrow and show Detective Culhane the list—"

But Flora was shaking her head. "No. That's not how we do things in my world."

So she was a gangster, too?

"We don't get the police involved," she added. "Never."

"Well, what do you suggest?" I asked. "We can't ex-actly go snooping around all these people—like Johnny Two Guns—trying to figure out who chews Beeman's pepsin gum!"

Flora frowned, her brows knitted. "What did you just say?"

"Didn't I tell you?" I glanced at Robert, who also looked baffled. "When I was in the alley, I found some chewed-up gum—Beeman's—stomped into some footprints that went nowhere. It was like somebody stepped out the back door of one of the buildings, spit out the gum—maybe shot your dad—and went back inside."

Robert pulled himself up straighter, and although he was in no shape to do much investigating, he did make a good suggestion. "We need to find out what's in the building that person came out of. Whether it's a store or an apartment. Who owns the place. That type of thing."

"Why?" Flora asked.

"Because"—Robert jerked his thumb in the direction of my composition book—"we might find out that Mike the Nose or some other guy on that list of your dad's enemies has a connection . . . or a key!"

CHAPTER 55

STOOD WAITING NEAR THE ALLEY WHERE CHARLES BESSE-mer had gotten shot, sifting the change in my pocket through my fingers. I'd worked hard to sell every one of my papers as quickly as possible, because I *supposedly* had a meeting.

Hunching my back against the cold wind, I peered down the dark, fairly empty street, wishing my ride would show up, and absently counted the coins.

Five cents. Ten cents. Mom's going to be happy . . .

"Hey, kid."

The voice I heard behind me was sort of familiar, but not in a good way. Or maybe it was the speaker's menacing tone that made the hairs on the back of my neck stand up.

Turning slowly, I faced the person who'd greeted me, and I greeted him back in a squeaky voice. "What do *you* want?"

CHAPTER 56

ALBERT ROWLAND DIDN'T HAVE HIS CLEAVER WITH HIM, and there was no bloodstained apron sticking out from under his short blue-plaid mackinaw coat. Yet he was still a menacing figure. His dark eyes glittered in the moonlight as he took a step closer to me.

I stepped back.

"You're the kid who came into the shop, right?" he asked. "Accused me of *murder?*"

Actually, I'd accused him of being a lousy father first, but I didn't point that out. My gaze darted to his hands, which were tucked into his pockets.

Could he have a gun in there? A knife?

My heart was racing, but there was no avoiding the truth. "Yeah. That was me."

In the split second I glanced down the street, hoping to see headlights, he stepped even closer. "Why'd you say that?"

"I . . . I don't know," I said, shrugging. "I say all kinds

of stupid stuff. Ask my mom!" That answer clearly didn't satisfy him, so I added, perhaps unwisely, "You're just so mean, leaving Robert, and you won't divorce Miss Giddings, and then Mr. Bessemer got shot . . . But I don't honestly believe you did it." That was a fib. I was really starting to think he might be guilty. I needed to save myself, though, and I lied even more. "Besides, I'm just a kid! Who even cares what I say?"

A reporter, that's who. But he didn't know that.

"Look, kid . . ." His hand darted out so quickly that I didn't have time to pull away. All at once, I was trapped. He twisted my wrist just enough to make it hurt. "You keep your mouth shut. I didn't kill anybody. And I don't need trouble with the law—or a bunch of mobsters! Understand?"

Nodding, I tried to pull away. Robert's dad was strong, though. "Sure . . . Sure, okay. I understand!"

"You don't say anything to *anybody*," he added. "Never even say my name again!"

"I won't!" I promised, peering down the street. *Where are they . . .*

"Kid!" Mr. Rowland squeezed my wrist, forcing me to look at him again. I met his cold eyes. "Like I said—I didn't kill anybody . . . *yet*. Got it?"

Oh, I got it. I started nodding like crazy. "I understand. I'll be quiet. I promise!"

Just then, as I was about to pee my pants, a long, dark sedan came rolling up to the curb. And although I suddenly wasn't sure I was going to be safer inside the auto, I tore free of Robert's dad and ran for a door that was opening so I could jump inside—where I immediately broke the promise I'd just made, to people I definitely shouldn't have confided in.

CHAPTER 57

WHO WERE YOU TALKING TO?" FLORA ASKED WHEN THE door was shut behind me. I thought she was concerned to find me getting harassed by a man on a fairly lonely street, until she added, "He was very handsome. Like someone I might meet in Hollywood!"

"That was Robert's father," I explained, settling into the back seat of the Bessemer's car. Nobody except Uncle Carl was up front, so it seemed like we had an actual chauffeur. Flora was so lucky, in some ways, with her pretty curls and her money and her acting career, even if two of those three things were what my mother would call "ill-gotten gains."

What would Mom think about me riding around in a bulletproof car with a gangster's daughter? How long till she finds out?

"What did Robert's dad want with *you*?" Flora asked, interrupting my worries—and making it sound as if nobody could ever want anything to do with me.

I rubbed my wrist, which still hurt. "For your information, he threatened to *kill me!*"

I shared that because I couldn't imagine how word about me blabbing would get back to Albert Rowland. It wasn't as if Flora would ever visit a store full of disgusting raw meat and talk to Robert's dad. But as usual, I hadn't quite thought things through. Uncle Carl had heard me too, and he swiveled around. "Why'd he threaten ya, kid?"

Fortunately, Flora's bodyguard also sounded more curious than anxious for me. I was pretty sure he wasn't going to seek out Albert Rowland either, so I told them both, "I went to his butcher shop the other day and told him he was a terrible father and probably killed Charles Bessemer too."

Uncle Carl's big, bald forehead furrowed. "Why do you think that?"

"Somebody besides Miss Giddings did it!" I said.

Uncle Carl stared at me for a long time, like he didn't know what to make of that. Then he twisted around to address Flora. "You getting out here?"

"No, it's too cold," she said. She waved her hand, indicating that he should drive on. "Take us around the corner. Down the street. Slowly."

Uncle Carl faced forward and steered the car away from the curb. "Why do you kids want to snoop around that alley, anyway?" he asked. "What's the idea?"

"I told you, we're not going *into* the alley," Flora

snapped at her uncle. "We want to see the buildings on *one side* of the alley. From the front!"

She really would be lucky if Uncle Carl didn't pop her one someday, even if he did lose his guardianship and a fortune because of it.

"Well, this is the street," Uncle Carl noted, driving slower. "What are you looking for?"

Noticing a white building, I leaned forward and tapped Uncle Carl's shoulder, which felt like rock. "Stop here!" I cried. "Right here!"

He did as he was told, pulling close to the curb again, and I could understand why Flora had a big head under her Frenchy beret. It was pretty nifty, telling an adult what to do and actually having him do it.

"See the building that's painted white?" I asked Flora, pointing to a structure that stood out from the other redbrick places on the block. "That's the one I was behind when you saw me by the trash cans."

Uncle Carl turned around again, and I was way too close to his big jowls. I could smell his breath, which was as bad as the first time I'd met him. Whatever he was combining with garlic, it was a terrible recipe. "What are you kids trying to prove?" he asked.

His voice was low, almost a growl, and I moved back, intimidated, while Flora ignored him. She rolled down her window, and I crawled practically onto her lap so we could both look, our breath making clouds in the cold night air.

Then we pulled our heads back inside, and I wasn't sure whether what we'd discovered was good or bad. But something told me it was good—for Miss Giddings, at least.

I met Flora's gaze in the dark car. "Looks like the place is . . ."

She seemed uncertain about what we'd found too, and she finished my thought in the form of a question.

"*Abandoned?*"

CHAPTER 58

I F THE BUILDING REALLY IS VACANT . . ." FLORA NOTED, SIT-
ting sideways, close to me, on the big leather seat.
Even so, I could only see her face when we passed under a streetlamp or another car went by. "If nobody
uses it . . ."

"It must be empty," I said. "There was an old For Sale
sign all curled up in the window, the whole place was
dark—plus the one pane of glass, by the door, was broken. Who could live with a broken window in Chicago
in the middle of winter? You'd freeze!"

Flora's eyes narrowed. "It almost looked like somebody'd broken that glass so he—or she—could reach
inside and *unlock the door.*"

I hadn't thought of that possibility. It made me begin
to appreciate being allied with the daughter of a criminal. I tried to think like a killer too, just to keep up. "And
the person who went inside could've slipped out the back
door and waited in the shadows for your father to come

into the alley . . ." I didn't describe the actual pulling of the trigger, but Flora understood.

She nodded, her corkscrew curls bobbing. "Yes! Then, afterward, he could've walked right back through the empty building and left, without the cops ever seeing or suspecting anything."

Flora and I blinked at each other, clearly surprising ourselves by actually figuring out a plausible scenario.

"I guess Robert had a good idea," I said, not wanting to overlook his contribution, even if he hadn't been able to come with us.

"Yeah, he's a smart kid," Flora conceded. "Too bad about his leg."

It was the closest I'd heard her come to being genuinely nice toward Robert, but I didn't want to make a big deal of it. She'd probably get proud of herself for being sympathetic and start bragging about that, too.

Flora was already done with Robert anyhow. She leaned forward and tapped Uncle Carl. "Where was my father going to eat, the night he . . . the night it happened?"

Sometimes Flora talked about her dad's murder as if she was hardly bothered, but sometimes she couldn't do that. I liked her better when she had trouble spitting out the words.

"Napolitano's," Uncle Carl said. "Where he always ate on Thursdays. The best place in town!"

I'd seen that restaurant before. It served Italian food and looked really ritzy from the outside.

"Did he always go through the alley?" I asked, understanding what Flora was getting at.

What if somebody had known Charles Bessemer's habits and lay in wait for him?

But Uncle Carl didn't answer me. "You kids shouldn't get messed up in this business," he said, for once giving *Flora* a suggestion. "Sure, your dad had some enemies. Everybody in this town does."

I wasn't so sure about that. Hardly anybody—except Detective Culhane, sometimes—really had it in for me. Well, and Robert's father, now.

"But the dame—Giddings—did it," Uncle Carl continued. "For once, the police are right."

"No. Miss Giddings didn't do anything," I protested. "And I'm going to prove it."

Uncle Carl snorted. "How?"

"I have evidence," I said. I had just told Albert Rowland that nobody cared what I said, but now I boasted, "And there's a detective and a reporter who actually listen to me!"

Okay, one of them listened.

If Uncle Carl had had a neck, he would've broken it, his head swiveled around so fast. "What kind of evidence?"

All of a sudden I wasn't sure I wanted to share more

with Flora's guardian. I was already in pretty deep with a mobster's daughter. Did I really want to get chummy with a man who was almost certainly a mobster himself? Because who knew what he'd do with my information?

"Aw, I don't really have anything," I said, slouching down in my seat. "I just want to help Miss Giddings, that's all."

"Well, she's going on trial in one week," Uncle Carl informed me. "I think it's a little late to help her."

I hadn't realized that the trial date had been set. I must've missed a story by Maude.

That wasn't much time . . .

Sliding down even lower, I nudged Flora, who'd gotten quiet. "Hey," I whispered, hoping Uncle Carl couldn't hear. "Why'd you get all strange when I mentioned the gum, back at Robert's? You about fell off of your chair!"

Flora's eyes got wide, just for a second. Then she said, softly, "I don't know what you're talking about. So just leave it be, okay?"

She *did* know and was keeping a secret from me. That didn't seem like something a good partner would do. Then again, I didn't understand everything about "her world." Maybe Two Guns chewed lots of gum, and she didn't want to mention that in front of Uncle Carl quite yet, in case he'd go shoot off Two Guns' nose too. Maybe the gum was something we'd discuss later.

"This is your house, right, kid?" Uncle Carl asked. I

hated how he never used my name, but I'd already agi-
tated him enough for one night, so I didn't correct him.

"Yeah, this is it," I said, reaching for the door handle.

Flora craned her neck to look past me out the window. "Wow. Too bad."

I might've held back from giving Uncle Carl a piece
of my mind, but I'd suddenly had about enough of Flora
Bessemer. "If we're going to be friends, you've gotta stop
saying stuff like that," I warned her. "Friends aren't . . .
mean!"

She took a moment to study me with those big blue
eyes. "Are we friends?"

I had no idea if she found that possibility completely
disgusting or if she—just like me and Robert—really
needed a friend. I preferred to think it was the second
choice. "Yeah," I told her. "I think we kind of are."

Before she could ruin the moment by opening her
mouth, I ran out the door and into my house, where I
read a note my mother had left about remembering to
turn off the lights and lock the door. Then I ate a few big
globs of peanut butter off my fingers, climbed into bed,
and tried to piece together all the things I knew about
the abandoned building, the gum Flora wouldn't talk
about, a gun that seemed to belong to nobody, and a lot
of complicated, strange relationships.

Detective Culhane and Maude.

Flora and her Uncle Carl.

Robert and his loony Aunt Johnene, who was so jealous of Miss Giddings.

Not to mention Miss Giddings and her not-exactly-ex-husband, scary Albert Rowland.

And especially the dead Charles Bessemer and *everybody*.

I must've been lying there about an hour before I realized I'd never fall asleep, and on what was probably a stupid impulse, I got up, got dressed in my warmest clothes, and sneaked out into the night.

CHAPTER 59

I WAS USED TO BEING OUT ON MY OWN AFTER DARK, BUT THE streets were really quiet as I walked through the city at about midnight. I mean, there were some people around, but not a whole lot, and I tried to stay in the shadows so nobody would notice me.

At one point, I heard loud laughter and music coming from buildings that didn't seem to have any lights on, and I wondered if it was one of the speakeasies I'd read about in the *Tribune*. Secret places where men and women went to listen to jazz music and drink bootleg alcohol, away from the police—until the parties got raided.

I wished I could at least see what a speakeasy looked like, but you had to have a password to get in, and be way older than ten, so I just kept walking until I reached the corner where I'd stand and sell newspapers later that morning, after the sun came up. Sunrise was still hours away, though, giving me plenty of time to explore the abandoned building, which I was trying to approach very casually, looking all around to see if anybody was watching before I slipped my hand through the broken pane of glass to twist the knob.

And the next thing I knew, I was inside.

Alone.

I hoped.

CHAPTER 60

THE BUILDING WAS DARK, AND THE ROOMS WERE EMPTY, SO every time I stepped, the floorboards squeaked like a dying mouse. And even though I came to expect it, the sound kept making my heart jump into my throat.

My palms were sweating too, although my stomach felt like it had a block of ice inside.

Sniffing the musty air, which smelled as if it had been trapped there for decades, I coughed, and that noise seemed to echo all through the place, from the cellar to the rafters.

Why am I here?

It's so dark that I can hardly see anything . . .

I forced myself to stand still, trying to rein in my imagination and control my fears. I kept picturing Albert Rowland looming behind me with his cleaver. But there was no way he could know where I was, and I pushed the image out of my mind. I also let my eyes adjust, until I could make out a few details in the room. White woodwork around arched entrances, white trim along the bottom of the walls, and . . .

Bending down, I peered at the floor and crept closer to where a shaft of moonlight came through a window, so a long, narrow section of the old boards was illuminated.

Squinting, I knelt to get an even better look.

The dust is disturbed, like somebody else *recently walked through* . . .

Just then I heard a noise coming from deeper in the building, toward the rear. Where the door to the alley would be.

For a second I froze.

Then a big shadow—at least it seemed big—stepped into the very room where I was crouching.

CHAPTER 61

I T WAS LATE, AND MOST OF THE TRIBUNE TOWER WAS DARK. But the city room was bright and bustling when I burst into it, completely out of breath and puffing the way Robert did.

The reporters who were working late all stared at me, again, as I made my way straight toward Maude's desk, where she was talking on the telephone. It hardly even surprised me to find her there. I had a feeling she didn't sleep much.

As I approached her, she got a worried, confused look in her eyes, and I heard her say "I'll call you right back, okay?" to someone on the other end of the line. Then she hung up the receiver just in time for me to crash into her desk and cry, "Somebody just tried to kill me! *Now* will you believe Miss Giddings is innocent?"

CHAPTER 62

I SABEL, ARE YOU *CERTAIN* YOU SAW SOMEONE IN THE BUILD-ing—where you shouldn't have been sneaking around late at night?" Maude asked, managing to express concern and chide me at the same time. "You're positive?"

"Yeth!" I told her yet again. I spit the butterscotch she'd given me—in an attempt to calm me down—into my palm so I could speak more clearly. "Someone was in there—and I barely got out the door!"

Actually, now that I was safe, I realized that I might've been exaggerating, just a little. I mean, I *had* seen a shadowy figure, and I *had* run to the door, but I honestly couldn't say whether anyone had chased me. It sure felt like somebody'd been breathing down my neck, though, as I'd fumbled with the knob.

"I'm pretty sure I nearly got killed," I added. "Probably by whoever killed Charles Bessemer. Maybe by *Albert Rowland!*"

Maude frowned. "Why would you think *that?*"

I had already done a terrible job of keeping my promise about not speaking Robert's father's name, so I told Maude, "He threatened me. Told me not to tell anybody I suspect him of murder!"

Maude's face got a little pale. "When you say he threatened—"

"He grabbed my wrist and said he hadn't killed anybody—yet." I repeated Mr. Rowland's not-so-subtle warning.

Maude didn't ask for more details. She reached for the telephone again while I watched, my eyes widening in disbelief.

Was she honestly going to finish her call after I'd just told her I'd been pushed around and then nearly murdered?

It seemed that way, so I popped my candy back into my mouth—then nearly spit it out again when a moment later she said into the receiver, "James? Can you meet me and Isabel now? Where Charles Bessemer was shot?"

CHAPTER 63

THERE WAS NO WORKING ELECTRICITY IN THE BUILDING I'D recently fled, so Detective Culhane switched on a big, heavy flashlight when he, Maude, and I went inside.

"Can I hold that?" I asked, thinking it would be fun to sweep the beam around the room, like he was doing. I knew Detective Culhane would never want a kid to do something just because it was amusing, so I added, "I could show you what I was looking at when the killer—"

"The *alleged shadow*," he corrected me, continuing to point the light all over the place, as though he was having at least a tiny bit of fun, in spite of grumbling about "wild-goose chases" over and over, ever since we'd met him on the stoop. Scowling, he held the beam on a big cobweb dangling from the ceiling, as if *that* might be a clue. "You're quite alive, so I don't think *killer* is the right word."

"James . . ." Maude's tone was cautionary.

"Oh, fine," he agreed, handing me the flashlight. "Tell

me everything that happened, so I at least can go home to bed—where you two should be."

He'd addressed both of us, but he was frowning at Maude. And there was an edge to his voice, as if the suggestion wasn't an idle one.

I held the beam low, in a way that let me see Detective Culhane and the reporter he was so obviously sweet on, without blinding them.

Did he worry about Maude running around the city at all hours, chasing murderers?

Was it something they'd talked about?

Maybe even something that *came between them?*

It seemed possible. Maude was shaking her head, just slightly, as if to say, *We've been over this.*

I wished I could see the expression in Detective Culhane's blue eyes better, so I'd know if there was frustration, or challenge, or both, there. Because all at once I felt as if I'd solved a different mystery.

He's afraid he'll lose Maude, just like he lost his wife, because she has a dangerous job that most women aren't even allowed to do. That's why they aren't together. At least, part of the reason . . .

"Izzie," Maude prompted, breaking what was becoming an awkward, charged silence. She took out her notebook. "Tell us what happened."

I eyed that pad warily. "Are you gonna write a story about this? Because my mother doesn't read the newspaper, but somebody will . . ."

Detective Culhane had been studying cobwebs again, but he turned on his heel and narrowed his eyes at me. "Your mother still doesn't know that you've involved yourself in a *murder?*"

"No," I informed him. "And she doesn't need to know. She's got her own problems."

He looked me up and down. "Yes. I imagine she does. One of which is about ten years old, and meddling—"

"Hey!"

"You two—enough!" Maude interrupted right before I stamped my foot. She pursed her lips and shot Detective Culhane another warning look, then spoke more softly to me. "Isabel . . . tell your story."

"Fine," I agreed, taking a few steps deeper into the building and shining the flashlight onto the floorboards. But the line of footprints was gone. Instead, the whole floor was disturbed, as if somebody had walked all over it. Or swept around the dust on purpose, by dragging a foot back and forth. "No," I groaned, looking up at Maude, who was most likely to believe me. "It wasn't like this before! I swear!"

Detective Culhane rubbed his eyes and sighed, but Maude seemed curious.

"What do you mean?" she asked.

I moved right to the spot where I'd knelt down, then I aimed the light at the floor. "This was lit by the moon when I was here before, and there were footprints, like somebody had shuffled through. But it was just a path. Now the whole floor's a mess!"

Detective Culhane stepped close to me and held out his hand for the flashlight. "I think we're done here—"

"James, not yet," Maude interrupted, placing a hand on his arm. I doubted many people got away with that. She pulled her hand away. "Izzie was threatened, too. By Albert Rowland. He implied that she would come to harm if she ever mentioned his name in connection with the murder again."

I thought Maude was putting things mildly. Robert's dad had threatened to *kill* me.

Regardless, Detective Culhane didn't seem surprised or worried. "I've looked into Rowland. He's a bully, but harmless."

"But—" I held out my wrist, which was bruised.

Detective Culhane spoke right over me. "He's got an alibi for the night of the shooting."

For a second I forgot that Mr. Rowland's having an alibi was bad for Miss Giddings. I was just pleased to think that Detective Culhane might've investigated Robert's father based on my suspicions. "You really talked to him?"

"That is my job, Miss Feeney," Detective Culhane reminded me. "Of course I spoke with him—and several people who swore they spent time with him at a supper club the evening Bessemer was killed. Rowland's story holds up. He was nowhere near the alley."

It seemed to me that a "bully" like Mr. Rowland might have liars for friends, but Detective Culhane had probably thought of that, too. I was pretty sure his inquiries had been thorough. Still, I had to ask, "So, if he's innocent, why threaten me? Huh?"

"Some people don't like being accused of killing a mobster," Detective Culhane pointed out. "The mob doesn't hold trials. They just *sentence*. Usually with gunfire."

Okay, I could see how Mr. Rowland might not want me shooting off my mouth about him being involved in a murder. "Oops."

"Oops, indeed." Detective Culhane looked at Maude and lowered his voice, as if that would keep me, who was two feet away, from overhearing when he said, "Maude, she's a kid—not a detective. I don't know why you've taken such a shine to her—"

Forgetting my recent mistake, I puffed up with pride. Had a shine really been taken?

"—but this is a game, in her eyes," he added, with a quick glance at me. "I'm sure Isabel has good intentions, but a homicide investigation is not a diversion for children. It's a *serious matter*. And nothing happened here."

I wanted to tell him again that I knew murder wasn't a game, but for once, I forced myself to hold my tongue as Maude worked her quiet, commanding magic.

"Give her five more minutes," she said. "That's all."

Detective Culhane opened his mouth, as if he was

going to keep arguing. Then he ran his hand through his hair, sighed, and took a step back. "Fine. Five more minutes."

For a second, I just stood there, until Maude made a rolling motion with her hand, urging me to hurry up and start talking.

"Oh, right," I said, recalling why we were in a gloomy building late at night. I pointed to the floor. "I was kneeling right here, examining what looked like footprints in the dust, when all of a sudden I heard somebody move, far back in the house. And before I could even get up —'cause I kind of froze with terror—there was a huge, dark shadow . . ."

I was starting to get caught up in my story, and I paused for dramatic effect, then pointed the flashlight beam directly at the pitch-black archway from which the massive form had emerged.

And just as I cried *"There!"* something came running out of nowhere and darted past us all.

Needless to say, I screamed bloody murder, and Maude jumped too. Right before she doubled over laughing.

As for Detective Culhane . . . he held out his hand again, palm up.

Shoulders slumping, I handed over the flashlight. "It wasn't a cat the first time," I grumbled. "It wasn't." I turned pleading eyes on Maude. "You believe me, don't you? And please stop laughing!"

She swiped a finger under her eyes and managed to

control herself. "Sorry," she said to both me and Detective Culhane. I thought she was mainly apologizing to him for dragging him out of bed for nothing. "It was pretty funny, though, you have to admit!"

Detective Culhane wasn't going to admit any such thing. "Come along. Let's go."

Without waiting to see if we followed, he strode toward the door, but I grabbed Maude's sleeve. "Maude?" I spoke quietly when she stopped and looked down. "You believe me, don't you?"

She stared at me for a long time. "I'm not sure, Izzie," she said finally. "Fear can change your perceptions. A suggestion can become a threat. A little cat can become a big shadow."

It wasn't the answer I wanted, but I was starting to appreciate that she was always honest with me. "Will you at least not write a story about this?" I requested. "Please?"

Maude hesitated, and I knew she was doing me a huge favor when she agreed. "Okay. Although it would've made good copy."

Yeah. It would've. "Thanks," I said. "I owe you one."

Then I let go of her arm, and we both went through the door that Detective Culhane was holding open for us. Outside, I looked around for the big police sedan, hoping for a ride home. It wasn't parked on the street, though, and Detective Culhane gestured toward a more modest automobile. "Come with me." He gave Maude another pointed look. "It's very late, and on some of the corners you'd pass to go home, there *are* far worse things than cats prowling around."

"I'm going back to work, James," she informed him firmly. "I have quite a bit to do."

"Of course you do," he said, opening the door for her. "Of course."

Oh, I had definitely figured out their whole relationship. Who said this stuff was too complicated for kids?

Then Detective Culhane opened the rear door for me, and I hopped inside. His auto was exactly as I would've guessed. Not fancy, but clean and comfortable.

We dropped off Maude first because we had to pass the Tribune Tower on the way to my street, where Detective Culhane stopped the car in front of my house. And although I needed to go inside and try to get a few hours of sleep before heading back out to sell papers, and I knew I was making a mistake, I couldn't keep myself from saying something that had been annoying me, just bubbling up like a blister during the whole, silent ride.

Sucking in a deep breath, I told the imposing, stern police officer who was already irritated with me, "You're nothing but a big scaredy-cat, you know that?"

CHAPTER 64

E XCUSE ME?" DETECTIVE CULHANE SAID, BENDING AND CUP-
ping his ear, as if he hadn't heard me right. "Did you
just call me a *coward?*"

All at once, I remembered how he'd fought in Europe, and I knew enough about him to be sure that he
hadn't curled up in his trench, crying—like, let's face it,
I would've done. I didn't like Detective Culhane most of
the time, but if a German grenade ever came rolling at
me, ready to explode, I'd want him by my side. Anybody
could just tell he'd throw himself right on it, without a
second thought.

"Not a coward," I said, regretting my strong words.
"But you *are* scared of something."

He turned around as far as he could, to see me better,
and arched his eyebrows. "Cats? Because *I* don't recall
screaming and doing a jerky version of the Charleston
when a *kitty* ran through the room this evening."

Okay, maybe I was starting to like him a little. He

could be funny, in a sarcastic way, which I thought was a sign of intelligence. And I appreciated smart people.

"If you'd been caught up in the story, like I'd been, and not gawking at cobwebs, you would've jumped too," I advised him. "But I'm not talking about cats."

He was tired and probably didn't care what I thought about him, but he was curious—another quality I admired. "What, then, Isabel Feeney?" he inquired. "What do you think I fear?"

When Detective Culhane stopped being so gruff, a person could appreciate how handsome he was, and I could see why Maude had fallen for him. And because I wanted her to be happy, I risked telling him, "I . . . I think you're scared to be in love with Maude because she has a dangerous job, and you might lose her, like you lost your wife."

His mouth set in a grim line—but he didn't dispute loving Maude. Instead, he asked, "Who told you I was married?"

I realized I'd said too much, and that I might get one of my few friends in trouble, but I had to confess. "Maude," I told him. "But only because I was prying into *her* life! Asking questions about you!"

Detective Culhane faced forward again, rolled his head back so that he was staring up at the roof, then sighed. But he didn't kick me out of the car, like I'd expected. "Oh, Isabel," he grumbled. "Of all the things you really shouldn't interfere with . . ." He turned and met my eyes again in the darkness, and he didn't seem angry. Just sad. "It appears that no matter what I say, you are going to gnaw on this murder investigation like a little dog that won't be dislodged from a pant leg. But my relationship with Maude is *really* none of your business."

"But . . . but she's sweet on you, too," I said, talking fast. I thought about how good Maude was with me. "And she'd be a great mother!" I added. "Remember how she got us in line when we were starting to fight?" I dropped my voice, trying to imitate Maude's calm but firm admonition: " 'You two—enough!' "

Detective Culhane sat still for a long moment. Then he rubbed his face with his hands and sighed again, staring straight ahead. And although he spoke my name, he hardly seemed to know I was there. "Isabel . . . you've no idea what you're saying . . ."

All at once I got a queasy feeling in the pit of my stomach.

Did I just stumble onto something else that keeps them separated? Kids?

Because the few women who have careers . . . They always quit when they have children.

And Maude loves her work . . .

"Maude Collier has fought hard to become the best reporter in Chicago," he said softly, confirming my suspicions without directly mentioning children or motherhood. "Her success is well deserved."

Okay. Maybe adults' relationships were a little too complicated for kids. Sure, I might've figured out the things that stood between a widower and a driven woman who loved each other. Things as personal as fear and as big as the rules everybody followed, which said that mothers—at least those who had husbands to support them—couldn't keep working. But I had no idea how people overcame those obstacles.

"Sorry," I said, starting to get out of the car. "I'm really sorry. For meddling. And everything."

"Isabel."

Detective Culhane's quiet voice stopped me, and I turned back, one foot on the street. "Yeah?"

"You're surprisingly perceptive for a young person," he admitted. "I can see, sometimes, why Maude wants to encourage your dream of being a reporter." I couldn't believe he was complimenting me. And had he spoken with Maude about me? Because I couldn't recall ever telling him that I wanted to be a journalist. Regardless, there was an inevitable *but*. "However," he continued, "while it appears that you are determined to clear your friend Giddings—although her fate is really in the hands of her attorney and a jury at this point—you won't stick your nose into my personal life, ever again. You won't inquire into it. You won't discuss it. You won't even *think* about it."

It wasn't a threat. It was just a fact.

I nodded. "Understood."

But I'd always be thinking about him and Maude now. Still, I promised, "I won't inquire, discuss, or think."

"Good."

Then I slammed the door and ran up onto my porch, where I found something I must've overlooked before.

An actual letter, for me, in a sealed envelope, halfway tucked under the mat I was supposed to use to clean my shoes. It hadn't come from the post office — there was no stamp or even address on the front — but there was my name, in flowery handwriting.

Hurrying inside, I opened the envelope with eager, clumsy fingers, unfolded a perfumed sheet of paper, and read:

Meet me at the prison tomorrow at three p.m. (That means "in the afternoon.") I want to speak with Miss Giddings.

And why don't you have a TELEPHONE?

When I read that insult, I knew who'd written to me even before I checked the very formal signature.

Sincerely, Miss Flora Bessemer

CHAPTER 65

WHY DO YOU NEED *ME* TO SPEAK TO MISS GIDDINGS?" I asked Flora when I met her at the appointed place and time. I'd given a newsboy named Jimmie two cents to cover my corner for a while, so I added, "And let's make this quick, okay? I gotta be back selling papers when the office jobs let out."

Flora eyed my fingerless gloves—her hands tucked all cozy in a white fur muff—and made a fake frown. "I don't know how you do that job! Working all hours in the cold!"

"Well, I don't know how you make yourself look so sweet in a bread advertisement," I shot back. "Because you can't be nice to save your life. Why would you think I don't know how to tell time? And it's not my fault we can't afford a telephone! My mother isn't a *gangster.*"

I'd unloaded a lot of stuff on Flora, from outright calling her nasty to reminding her that she lived in a family of lawbreakers, but she seemed to respect bluntness.

She didn't even fight back, and she ignored most of what I'd said. "I need you because you know how to get into the prison," she explained. "You said you've spoken with Miss Giddings." She glanced at the imposing structure behind us and made a shudder. What an actress! "I assume you come and go here all the time," she added. "Probably bringing things to people from your neighborhood."

Had we not just established that *her* family was made up of criminals? "You're the one who lives with bootleggers and people who get their noses shot off!" I reminded her. "The only time I came here, I was with Maude Collier!"

"Bessemers don't go to prison," Flora said, her nose in the air. "Father liked to say that we operate above the law."

"Above" the law? More like "outside."

And speaking of folks who probably belonged in jail . . .

"Hey, where's your big uncle?" I asked. "Why didn't he bring you here?"

Flora looked away and shrugged. "Uncle Carl doesn't frequent prisons, even socially. I'm not sure where he is."

She knew where he was, but she didn't want to admit that he was on some kind of mob-related errand, maybe for Al Capone. Why else would she refuse to look me in the eye?

Then she met my gaze again, jutted out her chin, and

challenged me. "So? Can you get us in or not? Because before she goes on trial for killing my father, I have a few questions for the woman who was *almost* my stepmother."

I thought about how I'd barely been able to get inside the Cook County Jail the first time, when I'd had Maude with me, and I started to tell Flora that even if "Morse" was on duty and remembered me, us getting five feet past the main entrance was unlikely.

All at once, though, I had a great idea, and I crossed my arms and cocked my head at Flora. "Just how bad do you want to get in there?" I asked her. "'Cause I think I can do it—if you'll do *me* a favor too!"

CHAPTER 66

FLORA AND I SAT ON A BENCH IN THE WAITING ROOM AT THE Cook County Jail, kicking our feet in awkward silence, while Morse—who *was* on duty again—kept one eye on us, as if we were trying to break out, as opposed to get in.

I checked the big clock on the wall. Its hands had been dragging around the dial ever since I'd hung up the telephone on Morse's desk after begging him to help me place a call.

Come on . . .

Then, just when I was starting to think something had gone wrong, Maude Collier swept in through the door, grinning from ear to ear.

"Well, hello, girls!" she greeted us both. But her wink was only for me, and although I'd recently dragged her to an empty house to see a stray cat, she wasn't being sarcastic when she said, "I can't wait to see how *this* truly brilliant plan turns out for all of us, Izzie!"

CHAPTER 67

MAUDE LED THE WAY TO MURDERESS'S ROW, WITH ME AND Flora trailing behind. Although it was warm in the jail, and very clean, Flora kept her hands tucked in her muff, as if she didn't want to touch anything in such a *filthy, despicable* place.

Did she really not see the irony?

"Will you stop acting like you're better than everyone here, Flora?" I suggested, waving at a killer named Clara Harq, whom I recognized from reading Maude's stories. If I recalled correctly, Mrs. Harq had bumped off her dentist husband—but she'd smiled at me, so I had to be nice, right? "Take your hands out of that stupid muff and act normal!" I added to Flora. "You wanted to come here!"

"Yes, well, I'm questioning that now," she said in her sniffy way. "And I don't know if I like having a reporter along, writing a story."

"That was the deal," I reminded her. "Maude gets us in, and you let her write an exclusive article."

That was the favor I'd wanted, not really for me, but for Maude, since I'd done such a bad job interviewing Flora at the funeral.

Flora wrinkled her upturned little nose as we passed another occupied cell, although nothing was stinky. "Yes, I know we agreed," she said. "But I don't think Uncle Carl would approve."

If she was trying to back out of our arrangement by threatening me with her gigantic "guardian," it wasn't going to work.

"I thought *you* were in charge of Uncle Carl," I noted. "And you're not going to lose your stupid movie contract. Even if you said something dumb, how would anybody in Hollywood see the *Tribune*?"

Maude glanced over her shoulder. I hadn't realized she'd even been listening, but of course she'd been eavesdropping, like any good reporter would've done. "You're going to look very sympathetic, Flora," she promised. Then she made up a mock headline, like I'd done the last time I'd visited the jail, even sweeping her hand the same way. " 'Young Girl Confronts Father's Accused Killer.' The public will eat it up."

That seemed so cynical. And yet, so true. I knew I would read the story when it was in print.

"Thanks for arranging this, Isabel," Maude added. "You really do have a nose for news!"

I started to blush, then forgot about the compliment, because we'd reached Miss Giddings's cell and . . .

Oh, poor Miss Giddings!

CHAPTER 68

WHAT ARE YOU ALL DOING HERE?" MISS GIDDINGS ASKED, rising from her cot and making a weak attempt at fluffing her curls. It didn't help. They were as flat and lifeless as her mattress, and she had dark circles under her eyes. She was far too skinny, too, and wearing a shapeless shift that made her look like she was a hundred years old. Frowning, she knitted her brows. "Isabel? And . . . *Flora?*"

"Hey, Miss Giddings." I clutched the bars of her cell and poked my nose inside. She still had some flowers, but most of them had wilted. "How are you?"

"I'm . . . I've been better," she said, her gaze darting among the three of us. "But I'm surprised . . ."

Maude didn't speak up to explain why we were there. She was busy scribbling in her notebook. Apparently she was going to let me and Flora run the show.

Fortunately, if there was one thing Flora Bessemer was good at, it was running shows.

"I had to see you before the trial," Flora said. She gave Maude a quick glance. "I've been reading about you in the newspaper, and I don't know what to think."

I backed up a step as Miss Giddings came to the bars and grabbed them too. Her knuckles were white. "You have to believe me, Flora—even if a jury doesn't—*you* have to believe that I didn't kill your father."

Flora stepped closer to the cell. "Why did you lie about having a gun? Because I read that."

Oh gosh, was Maude scribbling furiously!

"I *didn't* have a gun, anymore," Miss Giddings insisted. "I'd gotten rid of it. Given it to my sister, who lives in a rooming house with people who are practically strangers. I thought she needed protection—and I didn't want it around Robert."

My eyes were like saucers. "*Aunt Johnene* has the gun?"

Miss Giddings nodded. "Yes." She glared at Maude. "I've told the police—and reporters—that. I gave it to her months ago!"

Releasing my grip on the bars, I turned to Maude, confused. Was she holding back information that could help Miss Giddings? Because that would be terrible . . .

"How come you and Detective Culhane didn't mention that when you brought the gun to Miss Giddings's house?" I asked Maude. "That seems pretty important!"

"Detective Culhane wanted to see if Robert would voluntarily mention something about his aunt having the gun—and thereby corroborate his mother's story," Maude explained. "But Robert didn't do that."

I felt betrayed, and not just on Robert's behalf. "That seems kind of tricky!"

"Yes, I suppose it is." Maude didn't seem to think being "tricky" was bad, though. Still, she clearly knew what I was thinking. We'd talked about Aunt Johnene, and missing guns, and she'd kept something from me. "I'm sorry, Izzie," Maude apologized. "Sometimes detectives —and reporters—don't share everything they know until they're ready." Her gaze flicked to Miss Giddings. "And to be honest, I'm not sure I believe the story."

"I know you don't," Miss Giddings said softly. "You've made that clear."

"Your sister won't say anything about having a gun," Maude added to Miss Giddings. "She just said she's not surprised you wound up in trouble; then she slammed the door in my face. And the police haven't been able to confirm your assertion either."

Maybe Maude had reasons to doubt Miss Giddings's claims about giving away the gun, but she *really* shouldn't trust Aunt Johnene.

"Johnene Giddings is awful!" I reminded Maude. "I told you, she's a jealous, stingy person who practically makes Robert crawl just to get a bowl of soup. You can't trust anything she says. I swear, she wants Miss Giddings to hang!"

That last word . . . it seemed to echo through the

whole jail and was suspended in the air for what felt like eternity.

Behind me, I heard Miss Giddings suck in a breath, and when I spun around, she was resting her hand against her throat.

I grabbed the bars again. "It won't happen . . . I didn't mean to say it . . . It won't . . ." I'd been angry at Maude a moment ago, but now I looked to her for support. "Please . . . tell her . . ."

Although Maude Collier probably thought Miss Giddings should go to the gallows, she agreed. "Isabel's right. As I'm sure your attorney's also told you, pretty women always get off scot-free. I've seen it a hundred times."

"My attorney?" Miss Giddings finally smiled, but it was a wry, wan effort. "I can't afford a fancy lawyer. And the public defender is too overworked to worry about my case. He hasn't told me much of anything."

My heart sank. I knew enough, from reading the papers, to understand that being defended by a high-priced private lawyer was much, much better than having a public defender who was paid very little by the government to take cases for poor people. The public defenders were always overworked—and often lost in court.

Meanwhile, unlike most of the women accused of killing their men in Chicago during what was being called the "heyday of the murderess," Miss Giddings wasn't using jail to make herself look better. She was

wilting faster than the posies that suitors weren't send-
ing anymore.

Could I have even called her pretty right then?

"Please . . . please don't worry," I nevertheless begged.
"You'll be okay. Me and Flora and Robert are trying to
find the real killer, and we have some leads. Honest!"

Miss Giddings wasn't listening. She leaned against
the wall and buried her head in her hands. Her shoulders shook. "Please . . . everyone go now," she said,
her voice barely audible. "I'm very tired . . . Give Robert my love . . ."

But Flora Bessemer didn't get bossed by adults, and
she wasn't about to leave until she had the answers she
wanted. While Maude rested a hand on my shoulder,
indicating that it was time to go, Flora came right up
to the bars and asked a question that I certainly hadn't
expected.

"Just tell me . . . Did you love my father or not?"

Miss Giddings dropped her hands and slowly raised
her face to us. I could see tearstains on her cheeks, under her red-rimmed eyes, but her voice was steady, if
strained, when she informed Flora with a shake of the
head, "No, Flora. I didn't. Not the way I should have to
be his wife."

I looked at Maude, who for once wasn't jotting notes.
Her eyes were wide, and her hand was stock-still.

What the . . .

CHAPTER 69

SHE'S INNOCENT," FLORA DECLARED FLATLY, RIGHT BEFORE slurping the last drops of her chocolate egg cream through a straw, making a huge bubbling, gurgling sound. My stomach rumbled in reply, and I licked my lips, wishing I hadn't been too proud to accept Maude's offer to buy me a fountain drink. All I had was free water, which I'd insisted I really wanted. Flora pushed her tall, empty glass across the counter where she and Maude and I were sitting on stools that spun. "She didn't kill Father."

I noticed that since the funeral, Flora had never called her dad "dear Papa" again, so apparently that had all been for show. And although I was dying to know why she was so certain about Miss Giddings's innocence, I finally had to ask, "How can you talk about your dad getting killed and never really cry? Do you *ever* cry?"

Maude picked up her coffee and blew on the top, pretending she was more interested in not burning her tongue than in the conversation, but her keen eyes were studying Flora's face.

For her part, Flora was glaring at me, as if I'd insulted her. "Of course I cry. I just do that in private." She jutted her chin. "Bessemers don't cry in public!"

Bessemers sure had a lot of rules, and even if Flora could afford to pay for her own drink, I was glad I wasn't part of her clan. "You don't have to be so tough in front of your friends," I advised her. For some reason, I still kept trying to be pals. "I can't tell you how many times I wished I had a friend to cry with—about my father being gone, and lots of other stuff, too."

Flora jolted upright on her stool. "You don't have *any* friends?"

I gave her a funny look. "Do *you?*"

"I . . . I don't need friends," she stammered, reaching into the pocket of her velvet coat and pulling out a little beaded change purse. Opening that, she placed some coins on the counter. "I'm going to be in the movies. I'll have friends then!"

Maude and I exchanged skeptical looks over Flora's bent head.

Yeah, right! When you're rich and famous, you'll have real *friends! People will love you, just for who you are!*

"Flora?" Maude asked, smoothly picking up her pencil, so the movement was hardly noticeable. "You seem so certain about Miss Giddings's innocence now. Why? Especially since it seems as if you didn't really know her that well, and the evidence points toward guilt . . ."

"No, my father didn't bring her around too much," Flora agreed. "He was very private about things like that, and didn't always introduce me to his girl-friends."

"He had a lot?" I asked, thinking about how Johnene Giddings had claimed that Charles Bessemer had "approached" her first. "Lots of girlfriends?"

"I don't know!" Flora sounded exasperated. "I had a nanny when I was little, and Uncle Carl was paid to watch me too sometimes. I didn't really care if Father had girlfriends or thought about marrying again. I've never really needed a mother."

I started to say that everybody needed a mother, but when was the last time I'd really had one?

I mean, my mom tried, but she was so busy just keeping us afloat that there wasn't much energy left over for hugs and bedtime stories and whatever else mothers were supposed to do. "I guess I understand," I told Flora. "I kinda get by on my own too."

Glancing at Maude, I saw that she looked sorry for both of us—a newsgirl and a soon-to-be movie star. How often did *that* happen?

"Flora," Maude prompted. "About Miss Giddings's innocence . . ."

How had I forgotten that big topic?

"Yeah," I said. "How do you know for sure?" I swiveled

on my seat toward Maude, adding, "Like *I've* known, all along."

"Miss Giddings said that she didn't love my father," Flora informed us. "That's how I know."

Funny, because I thought that admission had made Miss Giddings look worse, and apparently Maude agreed.

"How does that prove innocence?" she asked, jotting a few notes. "I thought quite the opposite."

But Flora was shaking her head. "No. If she'd made a big show of pretending to love Father so much that she couldn't have killed him, I would've thought she was a liar and a murderess. She was being honest, though. She didn't love him that much."

"Not enough to kill him in a fit of passion," Maude mused, giving her pencil a thoughtful tap against her lips. "It is an interesting observation."

"Not just interesting," Flora said, pulling her empty glass close again and sucking down the very, very, very last drops before concluding, in her no-nonsense way, "It is correct."

"And you gotta admit," I added, "Miss Giddings isn't using her time in jail to fix herself up. She looks terrible. She's not wearing fancy clothes or getting her hair done nice."

"True," Maude conceded reluctantly. "But you don't know what her attorney is advising. Perhaps this is a new strategy to gain sympathy with the jury. Paint her as a fragile, damaged woman."

"Miss Giddings *is* fragile and damaged," I objected. "It's not just an act. Did you see how skinny she is? And if the men on juries"—and they were all men, no women allowed—"*always* acquit women who look pretty, why would an attorney try something different? Miss Giddings is beautiful when she's not in jail. Why wouldn't she use that to save herself from hanging—unless she was too discouraged and scared to fight?"

Maude didn't say anything. She just took a moment to consider what I'd said, which I thought was a good sign.

"She's not like the other women you've covered," I insisted. "She doesn't think this whole thing is a joke."

It was hard to believe that anyone could think murder was a laughing matter, but women in Chicago honestly did seem to believe that killing a man was pretty amusing, not to mention a way to get famous. Maude was always writing about how murderesses wanted to make sure they looked good in their newspaper photographs, and how they'd fight for reporters' attention in jail, hoping to see themselves in the papers.

"Miss Giddings isn't looking for publicity, either," I reminded Maude. "She doesn't ask to talk to you or beg you to take pictures of her. It's pretty much the opposite."

Maude still didn't reply, but that was okay. She was listening, at least. Then she looked between me and Flora as she placed some coins on the counter. "You are two very intelligent, observant, and determined girls. You really should be friends."

Well, I was trying. And since I'd gotten an endorsement from an attractive, stylish, and famous reporter, Flora looked at me more closely. Like she was finally starting to see past my shabby clothes and messed-up hair.

We all three got off our stools—Maude gracefully, Flora with a quick hop, and me practically tumbling because I wasn't used to sitting on chairs that spun. Needless to say, I didn't frequent a lot of soda fountains.

"I gotta go," I said, thinking that the kid I'd paid to watch my corner was going to be mad if I didn't get back soon. Plus, I was missing the people who would come out of their offices about then, looking to buy a paper for the streetcar ride home. "I'll see you two later."

"Izzie . . ." Maude grabbed my arm lightly. I looked up and saw apology in her eyes. "Again . . . I'm sorry if I kept something important from you or played a part in 'tricking' Robert. Sometimes I see things as a reporter and not as a friend."

"It's okay," I told her honestly. "I think I understand."

She let me go, and I started to walk toward the door. But before I got outside, Flora stopped me too, with a command, like I was Uncle Carl.

"Isabel Feeney! Wait!"

CHAPTER 70

WHAT DO YOU WANT?" I ASKED FLORA AFTER MAUDE LEFT us to go write up her big scoop about a beloved little bread girl's meeting with her father's accused killer. "And hurry up," I added. "I need to go sell papers."

"Oh, for crying out loud." Flora pulled her hands out of her muff and found her change purse again. "You and those *newspapers* . . ."

"What are you doing?" I asked as she dug among her coins.

"Here." She tried to give me a nickel. "Take this."

"I don't want your handouts," I objected, my cheeks flaming. It was one thing to accept some pie or a cab ride from an adult who knew how to be tactful about it, but quite another to get outright charity from somebody my own age. "I want to get back to my corner!"

Stamping her foot, Flora shoved the coin at me. "I'm just trying to be nice!"

I pushed her hand away. "You aren't very good at it!"

All at once, Flora's eyes got damp and her chin quivered. Not like at the funeral, when everything she'd said and done had looked fake, but for real. And although Bessemers might not cry in public, they apparently sometimes came awfully close. "Stop saying things like that!" she snapped. "Maybe you're not very nice either!"

I reared back. *Me, not nice? Me, who is trying to save Miss Giddings and Robert and missing selling papers to help HER?*

"What are you talking about?" I asked.

She sniffed, but not in a snooty way. "You're always telling me that I'm nasty and stuck-up and don't have any friends."

"Well, it's all true!"

"So are the things I tell you," she said. "Like about your house. So why is it okay for *you* to say mean things and not me?"

Gosh, maybe she had a point. "Sorry," I said. "It just seems different . . . And you never seemed bothered . . ."

Flora stared off down the street, her chin still quivering. "Well, it's not different. And I do get bothered." She hesitated. "I miss my father too. I *do* cry, sometimes."

"Hey." I waited until she looked me in the eye again. "Me too. I still cry too."

Me and Flora . . . maybe we would never be *great* friends. She was moving to Hollywood, for one thing. But Maude was right. We did have quite a bit in common, like brains and determination. But mainly, loss. Big, heartbreaking loss.

"Here." She handed me the coin again. "It's my fault you left your corner. Let me repay you, okay?"

I still didn't want the charity, but she was trying to be kind, and she probably didn't understand why I wouldn't want her money, so I held out my hand. "Thanks." Pocketing the nickel, I asked again, "What did you want to talk about?"

"Maybe Miss Giddings didn't love my father, but he cared about her, enough to want to marry her," Flora said. "And since I don't believe she's guilty—let's face it, somebody like the Nose probably killed him—I want to help her too."

"You mean by finding the real murderer?" I couldn't imagine Flora going out of her way to do more for Miss Giddings. Flora's main motive in trying to solve the case was to help *herself*—by getting revenge.

Maybe I was wrong, though. "Father would want me to look out for Miss Giddings," she said. "She was *almost* family, and Bessemers protect Bessemers."

"What can you do?" I asked. "I've done everything I can to convince Detective Culhane that he's got the wrong killer, but he says it's in the hands of the jury now."

"Yes, the jury of *men*, like you said," Flora reminded me. "Men who set pretty women free."

"I still don't understand."

"Just meet me at Robert Giddings's house tomorrow night," Flora said. "Whenever you're done working."

Then she dug another nickel out of her bottomless little change purse, which probably held more than my mother's big money jar, and pressed it into my palm so I could ride a streetcar back to my corner without getting chased off by a conductor.

I still didn't like handouts, but I accepted the coin, starting to understand that Flora didn't know any other way to make people like her except by flipping her curls around, batting her blue eyes, and paying them. Heck, her father'd paid her uncle to watch her.

I always thought that's what "family" did for free.

Hurrying off, I went to catch the next streetcar that was headed in the right direction, but I looked back once to see Flora flouncing down the sidewalk in her velvet jacket.

Yeah, she was helping Miss Giddings out of respect for her dead father's wishes.

But let's face it, she wanted to be part of what Robert and I were doing too.

Movies or no movies . . . she *needed* friends.

But what could she do at Robert's house that would sway a jury?

CHAPTER 71

BETWEEN FLORA'S "REPAYMENT" AND THE PAPERS I SOLD, plus the extra nickel I pocketed by *not* paying the streetcar fare, I was actually able to drop quite a bit of change into the money jar when I got home that evening. It made a satisfying clinking sound as it joined the other coins, and I knew Mom would be happy.

Then, as usual, I made a sandwich — cheese, that night — poured a glass of milk, and sat down at the kitchen table.

Taking a sip, wishing it were an egg cream, I noticed that my composition book and pencil were sitting there, forgotten, next to our salt and pepper shakers, which were shaped like Bonzo the Dog, from the cartoons.

Maude would never have left the house without her trusty notebook — and probably didn't have ceramic mutts on her table, either.

Why did she see any potential in me?

Swiping my arm across my lips, I wiped off my milk mustache.

And yet—I had a good memory. It seemed that I could recall the whole meeting between Flora and Miss Giddings. Pretty much every word.

Pushing aside my supper, I reached for the paper and pencil and, without thinking at all about what Maude might have written, began to put down what I hoped was an "Izzie" story.

Miss Colette Giddings, accused killer of Charles Bessemer, might be scared.

She might be wilting faster than the flowers that AREN'T coming to her cell anymore.

And she probably regrets ever accidentally getting engaged to a mobster.

But she sure as heck wasn't going to lie when the world's toughest orphan, Flora Bessemer, asked Miss Giddings if she'd been in love . . .

CHAPTER 72

NOBODY ANSWERED THE DOOR WHEN I GOT TO ROBERT GID-
dings's house, and if I hadn't seen Uncle Carl snooz-
ing in his auto, which was parked at the curb, I would've
thought I was too late. I'd had a long, if good, day hawking papers. A man named Marty Durkin, who'd killed a
federal agent in Chicago, had finally been caught after
leading police on a wild-goose chase all over America.
Everybody was grabbing the special edition of the *Trib*,
talking about Durkin—and how handsome he was, how
exciting the hunt had been, like he was a celebrity.

Maude had written the front-page, above-the-fold
story and had even interviewed Durkin at the train station before he'd been hauled off to jail in front of a crowd
of hundreds who'd come to admire a cold-blooded killer
and his new bride's jewels and furs.

What a fascinating life Maude leads.

What a sick city this is.

No wonder she thinks everybody's capable of murder!

I had a copy of the *Tribune* folded inside my coat. I should've returned it to the newsstand, but I knew there was another article, on page three, that also had Maude's byline: BESSEMER'S LITTLE GIRL CONFRONTS FATHER'S ACCUSED KILLER AT COUNTY JAIL.

I planned to read that as soon as I had a chance.

But first I raised my fist, ready to rap on Robert's door again. Then I pictured Flora not deigning to answer and Robert struggling to drag himself across the room, and I tried the knob.

Luckily, it turned, and I let myself in. Stamping the snow off my boots, I heard people talking upstairs.

"Hey, Robert?" I called. "Flora?"

Nobody answered, so I went up the staircase and down the hallway toward Miss Giddings's bedroom, where the light was on. There was a lot of noise coming from that room, as if somebody was moving stuff around. I could hear Flora's bossy voice, too, and Robert complaining about something.

Stepping through the door, I started to say, "Hey, you two . . ."

Then I saw the mess on the bed and on the floor and cried, "Why are you tearing apart this room?"

CHAPTER 73

I AM PICKING OUT MISS GIDDINGS'S NICEST CLOTHES," FLORA said, holding up a dress, scowling at it, and tossing it to the floor. "Creating outfits for her. Which we will take to the jail."

Dressing nicely was a strategy that women used to pull the wool over male jurors' eyes in Cook County. When Maude covered murderess's trials, she always mentioned how the ladies wore fancy hats, velvet chokers, and smart frocks when they took the stand to profess their innocence. Inevitably, the men all fell half in love and set the women free.

"Have you been reading Maude's articles?" I asked Flora, pushing aside some blouses that were scattered on the bed so I could sit down next to Robert, who was propped against the headboard. He smelled like he was using the VapoRub I'd left with him. "How did you know that clothes can help?"

"I've only read the stories about *my family*," Flora said,

inspecting a black wool skirt. She placed it on a pile with some items that I guess had passed muster. "I just listened to you and Miss Collier talking about how pretty women don't get convicted. And ..." She glanced at Robert. "I am sorry, but your mother is not looking her best!"

Robert frowned at me. "Isabel, is my mother okay? Because Flora makes it sound as if she's crying all the time, and scared ..."

"Of course she's scared," I told him. "But she'll be okay." I turned to Flora. "Can I help you?"

"No." Flora selected a navy dress with a bow at the throat. "You stick to snooping around trash cans. This is what I do well. I choose my own outfits for my advertisements, and I'm told I have wonderful taste."

We might've reached a little understanding the day before, but that girl could not stop insulting me—and complimenting herself—to save her life. Yet she had a point. I didn't even know what she was talking about when she pulled a fawn-colored dress out of the closet and mused aloud, "This twill would look lovely with a georgette hat. Robert, does your mother have one to match?"

Robert obviously didn't know much about fashion either. "I have no idea!"

Flora placed the brown dress on the pile with the other chosen garments, then rested her hands on her hips, studying her selections. "Well, I think this should do." She addressed Robert. "Your mother has lots of lovely clothes—for a clerk who can't afford a real lawyer."

He actually reached for his crutch, like he was going to take a swipe at her for insinuating that his mother's wardrobe had been bankrolled by her father. Then he settled back. "She's expected to dress nicely at Marshall Field's, and she gets a discount . . ." His face fell. "Although I suppose she's lost her job . . ."

For once, Flora didn't have a smart comment. She didn't say anything, and I stayed quiet too. I knew how quickly that cozy house would disappear—maybe right into Aunt Johnene's clutches—if Miss Giddings really didn't have a job. And if she spent much longer in jail . . .

I glanced at Robert's leg.

He can't sell papers, like me.

Can't do much of anything . . .

I shook off those concerns and focused on a more immediate problem. "Flora, picking out these clothes is great. But I don't think I can ask Maude to get us into the jail again."

"We don't need your friend this time," she noted. "We have someone else who is going to get us past the guards."

I assumed that Uncle Carl had finally agreed to visit a prison, and I was surprised to see that Flora was pointing at the boy who could barely move and sometimes could hardly breathe. "Him," she said. "Robert is going to get us in."

I was about to ask how that was going to work when Flora turned her blue eyes on me, adding, "And speaking of Maude Collier—did you happen to see the story she wrote about our prison visit?"

CHAPTER 74

BESSEMER'S ORPHAN CONFRONTS FATHER'S ACCUSED KILLER AT COUNTY JAIL

Little Flora Brave, Quiet

by Maude Collier

Flora Bessemer, best known as Chicago's be-loved "Bakery Pride" bread girl—now famous

as a murdered mobster's orphan—today confronted her father's accused killer at the Cook
County Jail, where Colette Giddings awaits
trial early next week.

"I had to see her," Flora said of the woman
who was nearly her stepmother—until a shooting in a dark alley took Charles "the Bull" Bessemer's life and stained Miss Giddings's white
ermine coat with blood. The young girl's gaze is
surprisingly steely. "I had to ask if she'd really
done it."

Ten-year-old Flora courageously accompa-
nied this reporter to the imposing prison, although while inside, she kept her hands tucked
in a fur muff, as if protecting herself.

Adored citywide for her charming smile in
advertisements that frequently grace the pages
of the *Tribune,* and soon to be famous nationally
for her planned appearance in a film with Marion Davies, Flora was stoic as she approached
Miss Giddings, who expressed wide-eyed surprise to have a diminutive, yet intimidating,
visitor.

"What . . . what are you doing here?" Miss
Giddings stammered, rising from her cot in cell
184.

Flora, maintaining admirable composure
—"Bessemers don't cry in public!" she claims
—cut right to the chase, asking the lady who'd
been found kneeling next to her father's body
and a gun, exactly why she'd lied to police about
owning a firearm.

Miss Giddings, pale and thin in a shapeless frock—a far cry from the fur she sported

while on Bessemer's arm—protested yet again that her gun was in the possession of her sister, Johnene Giddings.

The other Miss Giddings has steadfastly refused to corroborate that story.

Then the girl who is about to depart for Hollywood, but whose happiness at the prospect of stardom is diminished by the loss of her "dear Papa," as she called him at the funeral, asked the accused murderess point-blank, "Did you love my father?"

Miss Giddings's answer? A shake of the head and the admission, "No, Flora. I didn't. Not the way I should have, to be his wife."

The trial will begin Tuesday at the Cook County Courthouse.

Courthouse staff say they are bracing for a large audience to see the city's "prettiest killer" defend her life.

That was it. I lowered the paper, having read the whole article aloud to Flora and Robert.

I was frustrated because, in spite of the doubts I thought I'd raised back at the soda fountain, Maude hadn't changed her tone. Miss Giddings *still* looked guilty. And Flora came off as way too sweet, not counting her "steely" eyes.

But I wasn't really surprised. I understood now that Maude had years of experience working with murderesses and a different point of view from mine, and that she wouldn't write an article to please me, even if I'd made the whole interview possible. She'd just report the facts as she saw them. And nothing in the story hadn't really happened.

In a way, I had to admire that. And I was glad I hadn't been mentioned. That was Maude's favor to me.

Flora, of course, had mainly noticed how she'd been portrayed. She was beaming. "I like the part about me being brave," she said, oblivious to the fact that Robert had turned a completely new color. Green. As if he might vomit. "And she mentioned that Marion Davies will be in the film," Flora added. "Everybody will know it's a big production!"

I opened my mouth to tell her that her movie wasn't our main concern at this moment. Then I shut my trap. Coming to the house to help pick out clothes for Miss Giddings . . . that was probably about as selfless as Flora Bessemer got. I'd let her enjoy the nice publicity.

"Robert?" I asked. "Are you okay?"

"Just . . . just tell me," he said, rising up with effort to address Flora, not me. Although his breath was getting wheezy, the way it did when he was upset, he demanded — with determination that probably would've impressed his mean old father — "Tell me what I have to do to get us all in to see my mother. Whatever it is, I'll . . . I'll do it."

Flora nodded and sat down on the bed too, so we were like an honest-to-goodness team. Or, more accurately, part of the mob, about to plot our next crime.

We all leaned in as the daughter of a gangster looked between both of us and whispered, "Here's the plan . . ."

The funny thing was, I felt like the biggest criminal when I casually asked Robert a question as we were saying our goodbyes. I acted like I just wanted to make sure he had somebody nearby, since he looked pretty worn-out by the time Flora and I left, but I had my own reasons for inquiring, "Where's your Aunt Johnene live, anyhow?"

CHAPTER 75

THE TROUBLE WITH SNOOPING AROUND A BOARDING HOUSE is, it's hard to tell how many people live there. And who knows when they work or sleep or leave to, say, go shopping? I had to get into Aunt Johnene's room, though, and look for that gun, so I arrived real early at the address I'd pried out of Robert.

He must've wondered why I wanted to know the exact house his aunt lived in, but I'd avoided telling him that I sort of planned to break in. The last thing I wanted to do was cause more trouble for him if I got caught. The less he knew, the better.

"Come on, Aunt Johnene," I muttered, stamping my feet and hugging myself to ward off the cold. I was hiding behind an overgrown holly bush on the side of the shabby white house, watching as the ladies left for the day. So far, three young women, all dressed in skirts and high-heeled shoes and fashionable hats, looking like they worked in offices, had come giggling through the front door.

Did Aunt Johnene envy them, too, since she *wasn't* a secretary yet?

Did she ever laugh with the other boarders?

I doubted it. I couldn't imagine her being friends with the happy girls I'd just seen.

All at once I had a very exciting idea. What if Aunt Johnene kept a diary where she shared all her most jealous, awful feelings about Miss Giddings and Charles Bessemer and the women she lived with?

It seemed like something a bitter, lonely lady would do . . .

I was wondering all those things when the front door opened again and I heard footsteps on the porch. Then, lo and behold, Johnene Giddings strode down the steps in her stiff-backed, prim, purposeful way.

The only problem was, I still didn't know if there were other boarders around—or which room was Aunt Johnene's, if I did get inside.

I was trying to figure out what Maude Collier would do in my situation, when the best thing possible happened—although at first it seemed like the worst thing that could've gone wrong.

Right over my head, somebody opened a window, leaned out, and said in a surprisingly cheerful tone, "Why in the world have you been hiding there for an hour, you little spy?"

CHAPTER 76

ARE YOU SURE YOU WANNA HELP ME?" I ASKED THE VERY nice young woman, Dolores Siebley, who'd let me into the boarding house and was leading me up a set of creaky stairs right to Johnene Giddings's room. The whole place had that funny odor of cabbage I'd smelled on Aunt Johnene the first night I'd met her, and the atmosphere was pretty dreary, with lots of mismatched, old-fashioned furniture. But Miss Siebley seemed happy to live there. "I don't want you to get in trouble or kicked out," I noted.

"Oh, this is very exciting," my guide said, wrapping her bathrobe closer around her. She was a stenographer most days, but at home with an illness this morning—although she looked pretty healthy to me. I couldn't blame her for wanting a day off, though. I might've played sick once or twice in my life too. "I can't believe you're investigating a *murder!*" she added, looking over her shoulder at me, her eyes gleaming. "We all know Johnene's sister is in jail, but Johnene pretends like nothing's wrong."

I probably should've made up some fake reason for needing to get into Aunt Johnene's room, but I'd been so surprised when Miss Siebley'd popped her head out of the window that I'd blabbed quite a bit of the truth. But apparently, Aunt Johnene was unpopular enough that at least one of her housemates didn't mind letting her possibly get drawn into a murder case. Miss Siebley didn't even seem to care that I was only a kid, maybe because I'd mentioned that I had a history of helping Detective James Culhane, Homicide Division.

He'd love that, if it ever got back to him!

We had arrived at the landing, and Miss Siebley sighed and shook her head. "What type of person doesn't help her own sister—and a poor, crippled boy?" Then she reached for a doorknob and twisted it. "Well, here you are. I don't know what you'll find, but if it helps that sweet woman I've seen in the newspapers get out of prison, that's just wonderful. It's so hard to believe Johnene has such a lovely sister. Colette looks so sad in the photographs!"

"Are you reading Maude Collier's articles?" I asked, confused. "In the *Trib*?"

"Yes," Miss Siebley confirmed. "All of us girls are—when Johnene's not around. It's so thrilling!"

I finally understood why Maude could go overboard

trying to make her readers see that murderesses weren't all wonderful—even if she was wrong about Miss Giddings. In spite of all the things Maude had written to make Miss Giddings look guilty, Miss Siebley still thought she was "lovely."

"I guess I better hurry up," I said. "I don't want to get caught nosing around here."

"Don't worry. Johnene should be away most of the day," Miss Siebley assured me. "Secretarial school is serious business!"

"Oh, good." Feeling a little less nervous, I entered the room, which was very sparsely decorated. The single bed was neatly made, the patchwork quilt on top perfectly smooth, and there was nothing but an empty water glass on the nightstand. The closet was narrow and the chest of drawers small. It certainly wouldn't take long to go through everything. Yet reaching for a drawer, I hesitated. I had no right to touch Aunt Johnene's things. Then I pictured Miss Giddings going to the *gallows,* and Robert crying and alone—not to mention Detective Culhane holding a bunch of undergarments, as if he hardly cared. Maude wouldn't have thought twice about nosing around either.

Pulling open a drawer, I gingerly rooted through some personal items of the nature that Detective Culhane had handled. Except not as frilly.

"What are you hoping to find?" Miss Siebley asked,

craning her neck so she could see from where she was leaning against the door frame. "Something in particular?"

I wished she would leave me alone, but clearly she wasn't going to miss a thing. "I'm not really sure," I said. I didn't want to alarm her by mentioning a gun. "I thought she might keep a diary . . ."

"I don't have a diary."

My whole body froze. And when I turned slowly toward the bedroom door, I saw Miss Siebley pinned against the frame, her eyes wide and one hand over her mouth, as alarmed as I was to find Johnene Giddings standing in the corridor, arms crossed, mouth a thin line, and fury in her eyes.

"I wish to speak to Robert's friend," she said in a low growl. Stepping into the room, she addressed her housemate but glared at me. "Leave us alone, Dolores." I was already terrified, but my knees really started knocking when Aunt Johnene added, *"And close the door on your way out."*

CHAPTER 77

I SHOULD CALL THE POLICE," AUNT JOHNENE THREATENED, stepping closer to me. I was already trapped against the bed, so all I could do was lean back. She stuck her finger right in my face, her eyes the merest slits. "You have no right to be here!"

I was scared, but I noticed that she wasn't rushing to call the cops. "If they come here, *they'll* start asking about the gun again," I warned her. "They'll poke around too!"

"*I'm* not under arrest," she snarled. "I'm not even a suspect!"

"Maybe you should be!" I snapped. She was starting to make me angry, wagging that finger around and acting like she was perfect, when really she was the opposite. "You're jealous of Miss Giddings, and you probably shot Charles Bessemer—or tried to kill your own sister! You want that house—and a husband—so bad!"

Of all the rash things I'd said, that was probably the

most reckless rush of words to come spewing out of my big mouth. Aunt Johnene bent down even closer to me, so my knees buckled against the mattress and my backside thudded down onto the quilt. She probably wasn't happy about me messing that up, either. "Get out of here," she growled through gritted teeth. Her voice was quiet, though, no doubt so Miss Siebley, who was probably right outside the door, wouldn't hear her tell me. "And you watch yourself, young lady. People like you, and Charles Bessemer, and my sister, who go out looking for trouble . . . You might just wind up dead in an alley or at the end of a noose too!"

CHAPTER 78

I WANTED TO TELL MAUDE OR DETECTIVE CULHANE ABOUT how Aunt Johnene had threatened me, just like Albert Rowland had done, but by the time I was done selling papers, it was pretty late. I was also sure that Detective Culhane would tell me I deserved to be chewed out. And even if I found Maude at the *Trib*, which was possible, she might not approve of what I'd done either.

Or would she think I was brave and enterprising?

Regardless, I decided to go home, and I let myself in to my dark, empty house.

At least I thought nobody was there, until—before I could even turn on a lamp—somebody who was sitting in the shadows asked quietly, "Who in the world is Maude Collier, Isabel? And what does she want with you?"

CHAPTER 79

SHE . . . SHE'S A FRIEND OF MINE," I TOLD MY MOTHER, WHO had waited for me in our worn armchair with an envelope in her hands and a deep frown on her face. "I met her . . ." How could I explain it without mentioning the murder? "I met her while I was selling papers," I said vaguely. "She's a reporter for the *Trib*. A really good one!"

My mom didn't know much about my job, and she must've believed that reporters and the kids who sold newspapers on street corners mingled all the time. She didn't question my explanation. But she still wasn't happy. She tapped the envelope against her palm, clearly trying to stay calm. "Did this Maude Collier take you to a *prison*, Isabel? Because it seems as if you wrote a story about visiting a killer in the county jail!"

My mouth got very dry. "Is that what's in the envelope?" I asked with a nervous glance at the letter. "That dumb thing I wrote?"

"Yes, Izzie," Mom confirmed. "There's a story in your handwriting, all marked up, and a note from your 'friend'!"

"Oh gosh, Mom!" I forced a smile, acting like she was being silly, worrying about me. Stepping closer, I held out my hand and told a pretty bad lie, only so she wouldn't get more upset. "I didn't *really* go to the jail. Do you think they'd let kids in there?"

I saw uncertainty in my mother's eyes, but she didn't give me Maude's note. "I still need you to explain this."

I took just a second to formulate a new fib, then said, "Sometimes I take the facts in Maude's . . ."

My mother gave me a funny look, and I quickly changed that to, "I mean, I take Miss Collier's articles and rewrite them in my own way. She wants to help me with my dream of being a reporter. She's really nice."

There were a lot of holes in that story—because half of it wasn't true—but my mother didn't seem inclined to ask me more about the article itself, or the jail visit. She mainly looked pained, as if I'd said something to hurt her. Her forehead was all furrowed, and the lamp she'd turned on, next to the chair, made her fine hair a frizzy halo. "You . . . you told this woman that you want to be a reporter?" she asked, studying my face. "Really?"

"Yeah," I said. "She thinks I can do it too!"

I thought Mom was upset because I was interested in doing a job mainly done by men. Or that she believed I was setting a goal I'd never reach. But when she lowered her head and muttered, "I didn't know that, Isabel. Didn't know you dreamed of things like that . . ." I realized that she was hurt that I'd confided in another adult. A woman. And an obviously accomplished, educated one at that.

All of a sudden I was hurting too. For her. "Hey, Mom . . ." I knelt down in front of her chair, trying to see her face. "It's just a silly dream . . ."

"No, it's not silly," she said, smoothing the envelope on her lap, as if it were no longer evidence of me sneaking around to prisons, but something precious. Her head was still bent, so I couldn't tell for sure, but I was afraid she was crying. "It's a lovely dream, Isabel. One your father would have been proud of. I hope this Miss Collier can help you achieve it."

My eyes got a prickly feeling that I hated, and I didn't know what to say.

Mom finally raised her eyes, and they were rimmed with red, the way Miss Giddings's had been. "Miss Collier mainly said your work was very good," she told me, quietly. "She says you have talent. And from what I read, you do have your father's way with words. He would be so proud of you."

We got silent then, both of us probably thinking how different tings might have been if Dad were alive. I really wanted to hug my mother. But I couldn't quite bring myself to do that. It was almost like I was afraid. If I wrapped my arms around her, I'd feel how fragile she really was. How close to completely breaking. And she didn't hug me, either. She just patted my arm. "You should get some sleep, Izzie. It's very late."

I stood up, taking the envelope with me. "Hey," I said, finally realizing that it was strange for her to be home and in a housecoat. Worry tickled my stomach. "How come you're not at work?"

"My hours were cut back," she informed me. "I'll have two evenings a week off now."

That was the best and worst news imaginable. My mother desperately needed a rest. But we desperately needed *money*, too. I tried to make it seem like a good thing, though. "That's great," I told her. "You shouldn't have to work all the time."

She tried to smile as if she agreed. "Go on to bed, Isabel," she urged. "I'm going to stay up for a while. I'm not used to sleeping at night."

"Okay. Good night."

My mother planned to be awake, but she reached up and turned off the light, probably to save a few pennies on the electric bill, so I felt kind of guilty when I went to my room and switched on my bedside lamp. But I just had to know what Maude had said about my story. Yet as I read her comments, which were mostly encouraging, I kept wondering why I was able to come up with ideas to help Miss Giddings but I couldn't seem to help my mother, to save *both* our lives.

CHAPTER 80

THE GUARD NAMED MORSE ROSE FROM HIS CHAIR WHEN Flora and I dragged a big suitcase full of Miss Giddings's clothes through the doors at the Cook County Jail. "Oh, no," he said, wagging a finger. "Not again . . ."

But he stopped protesting and let his jaw hang open when he saw that we had a new kid along with us. A boy who was hobbling across the floor, dragging his left leg, and huffing so much that I was honestly afraid he might keel over. But Robert Giddings was determined to see his mother, and he had refused to turn back, even when Uncle Carl had practically insisted.

Of course our chauffeur had obeyed Flora, who didn't seem worried about Robert at all. "Just drive," she'd ordered her uncle.

And Flora wasn't intimidated by Morse, either. She stepped up to the desk and batted her eyelashes, using her little-girl charm, which didn't quite mask the threat in her words. "You're not going to turn away a boy who can barely walk or breathe, thanks to polio, after he's dragged himself all the way here to see his poor mother on the eve of her murder trial, are you?" she asked, crossing her arms over her chest. "Are you really going to send a crippled kid home without even letting him hug his mama—who might be *hanged?*"

CHAPTER 81

THAT 'MAMA' STUFF IS SICKENING," I ADVISED FLORA, WHO was leading the way through the jail. Although Robert had two crutches, I kept one hand on his elbow. Flora had convinced Morse that we were both needed to help him—not that *she* was doing anything to prop him up. Her hands were in that fluffy muff again. I was dragging the suitcase, too.

I had to give Flora Bessemer credit, though.

She'd been right. Nobody could deny a kid who'd had polio a chance to see his mother before she might get sentenced to death. And apparently nobody could deny anything to an orphan whose father had been murdered. Especially an orphan who happened to have blond curls, blue eyes—and a pretty forceful personality.

Of course, Morse hadn't been sympathetic to me. Flora'd just convinced him that I was a "strong" girl, "used to hard labor," whom Robert could lean on when necessary.

Getting irritated with her in spite of how well her plan had worked, I added, "Nobody over five years old uses 'mama'!"

"Oh, adults love it when children use 'mama' and 'papa,' " she said, pulling one hand from her muff to wave it at me dismissively. "I use it whenever I want to appear weak or helpless."

"Why . . . would you want to do . . . *that?*" asked Robert, who *was* weak and helpless.

"To get what I want," Flora informed him.

Robert wasn't listening. He'd broken free of me and managed to pick up the pace, his brace squeaking in a quicker rhythm as he hurried down the corridor. And I guess I was wrong about kids our age avoiding the use of childish nicknames. Before *I* spotted Miss Giddings, Robert cried out, "Mama!"

CHAPTER 82

I DON'T THINK CLOTHES WILL HELP," MISS GIDDINGS SAID AS Flora held up something called a "silk crepe" dress, which sounded to me like a dessert you'd eat in France. A nice guard had opened the cell so Robert could lie down on the cot. He was wheezing something terrible, and Miss Giddings was distracted, fussing over him. She hardly seemed to care about the clothes, and she bent to smooth her son's hair again. "Robert . . . why did you come here—"

"Look, he's here already, so why don't you pay attention to these outfits?" Flora interrupted. "You need to look good for the trial."

Miss Giddings sank down on the bed and rested one hand on Robert's bad leg, as if she needed to be connected to him. I hated the lack of spark in her eyes and the defeat in her voice. "The evidence all seems against me," she reminded us. "I don't see how a nice skirt or some hose will do anything."

"A nice skirt can do everything!" I said. "Don't you ever read those newspapers I sell you?"

"Yes, but . . ." Her gaze remained locked on Robert.

"Haven't you read Maude's articles about how women who dress nice don't get convicted?" I continued, remembering one case in particular. "Didn't you read about how Sabella Nitti came to court in ripped stockings, with no makeup on, and got convicted of murder? Then, when she got a second trial, she put on lipstick and a pretty dress, and now she's free. Maude wrote all about it!"

In fact, Maude had seemed very frustrated by Mrs. Nitti's overturned death sentence.

"Maude's always writing about how women use the jail to spruce up," I added. "And they all win their cases."

Miss Giddings stroked Robert's braced leg, growing thoughtful. "I have heard the other women talking about how important appearance is for a trial. But it seems so . . . *manipulative*. And wrong."

Flora rolled her eyes. "Oh, please! How is it any different from putting on these same clothes to sell a man a suit at Marshall Field's?"

Miss Giddings's cheeks flushed. Let's face it—she'd not only sold Charles Bessemer some clothes, she'd snagged him, too. Maybe away from her sister.

As if any man would ever stick with Aunt Johnene once he got to really know her. I pictured the rage in her eyes as she'd confronted me in her room, and I suddenly confessed, "I . . . I tried to find the gun—at your sister's house, Miss Giddings."

"I knew you were up to something when you asked for her address!" Robert cried in a rare show of energy.

Miss Giddings leaned forward, her hands clutching the edge of the thin mattress. "How . . . And did you . . . "

I shook my head. "No, I didn't find it. But your sister caught me snooping in her room—another boarder let me in—and Aunt Johnene told me I'd be lucky if *I* didn't end up dead in an alley!"

"You sure aren't afraid to stick your nose in everybody's business," Flora noted, pulling another dress out of the case. I couldn't tell if she thought my being a busybody was a good or a bad thing. "I hope you at least *learned* something."

"No, I didn't. Except that I should 'watch' myself." I shot Miss Giddings a guilty look. "Sorry."

Miss Giddings grew even more solemn—not only because I'd failed to be of any help. "Oh, Johnene." She wasn't angry or accusing. Just wistful. "She's been jealous of me since we were little girls, and it has twisted her up inside. She probably thinks she's doing right, refusing to cooperate."

I didn't understand. "How so?"

"I think Johnene has truly come to believe that I'm wicked and deserve punishment," Miss Giddings explained. Her cheeks reddened again. "And perhaps I was

wrong to see Charles when I knew my sister liked him."
She averted her gaze, looking out through the bars.
"That wasn't very nice of me . . ."

"She should still help you," I said. "I mean, Mr. Bessemer never would have stayed with *her!*"

Miss Giddings smiled wryly. "I'm sure Johnene doesn't
see it that way." She grew serious again. "Please be careful, Isabel. Don't get *yourself* in trouble over me."

"I won't," I promised, although I felt like I was already in some trouble—with both Aunt Johnene and
Robert's father. "But you've gotta do everything you
can to help yourself," I told her. "You're innocent. It
might not be fair that a bunch of guilty women have
walked free just because they're pretty, but you didn't
hurt anybody. Please, pick out a good outfit for your
trial."

Robert was breathing steadier, and he pulled himself
more upright. "You should listen to Isabel," he urged
his mother. "She reads the papers and knows a lot." He
glanced at Flora and offered her a grudging compliment too. "And Flora seems to know about how to dress
nicely."

"I choose my own outfits for Bakery Pride, and I've
modeled for L'il Miss and Mister, too, for their advertisements," Flora said, heaping more praise on herself. As
if we hadn't already heard the part about the bread, or
needed to know that she'd also trotted around preening

for a store where rich people bought their kids' clothes. "Just let me help you."

Miss Giddings frowned. "Flora . . . why do you want to help so badly? Are you that certain I didn't kill your father?"

"Yes, I am," Flora confirmed, offering Miss Giddings the silk crepe dress again. "And I think you should wear this. The shade of brown goes well with your eyes, and the cut will make you look fashionable, but will show that you take the trial seriously, too."

"That *is* pretty nice," I said, adding my two cents.

Miss Giddings hesitated, then rose. "Okay." She had more color in her cheeks and a tiny bit more spark in her eyes. "I always did love this." She took the dress from Flora and held it up to herself, smoothing the fabric against her gaunt frame.

I was worried that she might be too skinny to pull off the outfit, but I said, "You're gonna look really pretty." Hesitating, I added nonchalantly, "You might wanna eat something between now and the trial. Just to keep your strength up."

"I brought you matching shoes," Flora noted, rooting in the suitcase for a pair of stylish pumps. She set those on the floor. "And do your hair up. Your curls are as frizzy as Isabel's."

"Hey . . ." I started to protest, but my hair *was* a mess.

"There's a woman in cell one fifty seven who used

to be a hairdresser," Miss Giddings said. "They say she stabbed her husband, but she seems very nice to me. I'm sure she'll help me."

I hoped the lady in cell 157 didn't have to use scissors on Miss Giddings.

Apparently Miss Giddings wasn't worried about that. She had turned her attention back to Robert, who was being his usual quiet self. Maybe even more silent than normal. "You should get home now, Robert," she urged him. "I don't want you to overdo it."

Looking at Robert, I realized it was a little too late for that. He wasn't getting blue, but he had very dark circles under his eyes. And we had a long way to go, just to get him back to the automobile. "Yeah," I agreed. "We should get going."

Robert nodded, and Miss Giddings helped him stand up. They wrapped their arms around each other for a long time, the way they'd done when we got to the cell. Long enough that I—and even Flora—looked away to give them some privacy.

Then Robert took his crutches and we started our slow way out of the cell, which a guard quickly locked, making an awful clank. Before we were five feet down the corridor, Miss Giddings called after us.

"I love you, Robert. Please don't worry about me."

He stopped and stiffened, then turned slowly around, but he didn't say anything. I was pretty sure he was trying to keep from crying.

Then Miss Giddings looked at me. "Has anyone approached you about testifying yet, Isabel? You know you have to testify, right?"

It was my turn to freeze in place.

How had I forgotten *that?*

CHAPTER 83

I THOUGHT YOUR MOTHER LOOKED PRETTY GOOD," I FIBBED
to Robert, who was next to me in the back seat of Uncle Carl's big sedan. I was starting to get used to the bulletproof quiet—and to having an adult drive me around.
Too bad Robert wasn't more comfortable. Although the
auto had a heater, like Detective Culhane's police car,
the cold was starting to bother his lungs again. "She sure
seemed happy to see you," I added. "Probably the happi-
est she's been in jail."

"She . . . she was worried," Robert said with effort. "I
made her more worried . . . by going."

Flora was riding in the front seat, and she turned
around. "You got us into the jail, and now your mother's
going to look better for the trial. You *had* to do it. She
couldn't go before a jury in some old housedress!"

"Thanks . . . Flora," Robert said.

Maybe they would've been fine as siblings after all.

Or maybe not.

"Did I hear you say you're gonna testify, kid?" Uncle Carl asked. His jowls were, as usual, flapping, and his breath, like always, smelled terrible. "You're a witness?"

I assumed that I was the "kid" in question since I had been fretting about taking the stand. "Yeah, I guess I'm testifying," I told him. Then I sank down in the seat. "I don't know how my mom's not gonna find out about *that*."

"Cat's . . . out of . . . the bag," Robert managed.

"Gee, do you think so?"

"Why do they want you on the stand?" Uncle Carl snorted his bulldog laugh. "What can *you* tell anybody?"

"I was first on the scene," I reminded him. "And since then I've been investigating. I have all sorts of things to say."

"Oh, yeah?" He glanced over his shoulder, his eyebrows arched. "What kind of things?"

"Well, I went back to that building you drove us to and found footprints in the dust. And I searched the alley, too, and found clues in the snow, including—"

"Isabel!" Flora cut me off abruptly. "The lawyers and the judge won't let you just talk, you know. You're only allowed to answer questions at a trial. You can't just say anything you want."

I leaned forward. "How do you know about trials?"

Flora shrugged. "Everybody knows how trials work."

Robert and I shared a look that said, *Maybe everybody who grew up with gangsters!*

I sat back in my seat. "Well, I'm gonna say everything I want to say, even if I have to do it fast, and nobody's gonna shut me up until I'm done."

"The judge'll shut you up," Flora predicted. "And the lawyers."

Why was she suddenly not on our side?

"Don't you want me to tell about—"

Flora spun around again, fast. "I'm just telling you that you're only supposed to answer the questions, or the judge will *shut . . . you . . . up.*"

"All right, all right," I grumbled, crossing my arms. "You don't have to get all snippy about it."

We rode the rest of the way to Robert's house in silence. For some reason, I felt uneasier than usual for him when we left him to nap on his couch.

And I got even more anxious when I got home, where there was yet another envelope waiting for me, stuck in the crack between the door and the frame.

A letter that I was really glad my mother hadn't seen, because it was marked "Official Summons."

Yup. I, Isabel Feeney, was gonna get on that stand and defend Miss Giddings's life. And no matter what Flora said, nobody was gonna *shut me up.*

Or so I thought.

CHAPTER 84

I T WAS SNOWING THE NIGHT BEFORE MISS GIDDINGS'S TRIAL
started, and the city was strangely quiet, as if everybody were holding their breath, worried for her.

I knew that wasn't really true—in fact, the people
who were even aware of the case, thanks to Maude's articles, either didn't care at all or were excited to see a
pretty young woman fight for her life. Trials were big entertainment in Chicago, not unlike mobsters' funerals.
Lots of folks considered the courthouse a theater, where
they could go see live drama for free. Not too long ago,
when two rich kids named Leopold and Loeb got tried
for killing another boy just for the thrill of committing
murder, the courtroom hadn't been nearly big enough
to hold everybody who wanted to get a seat.

*No wonder the rest of the country thinks Chicago is the
murder capital of the world.*

Bending, I picked up the small stack of newspapers
at my feet, giving up on selling them for the evening.

The snow was falling harder, and the few folks walking by had their heads bent down and their collars pulled up against the storm. Nobody was stopping to buy a *Tribune,* and I needed to get home and sleep. I had to be at the courthouse early the next morning, since a witness could get called at any time.

I guess I have to tell my mother what's happening.

Sighing, because I was going to be in big trouble and my mother would have more to worry about, I tucked the unsold papers under my arm, once again glimpsing Maude's story about Miss Giddings's trial. The article —JURY TO DECIDE IF IT'S NOOSE FOR "PRETTIEST" SLAYER—was small, but it was on the front page, and there was a picture of Miss Giddings from when she'd first been arrested. She looked really pretty, if wide-eyed.

Hunching my shoulders against the wind, I started tramping through the snow, heading back to old Mr. Rozzoli's newsstand to return my extra *Trib*s. But after I'd gone about ten yards, I stopped, right at the end of the alley where Mr. Bessemer had gotten shot.

It was a potential shortcut, one I sometimes used to use, but it had always made me a little nervous. And I definitely hadn't passed through after dark since the murder.

What's wrong with you, Izzie? Are you that scared of Aunt Johnene or that big bully Albert Rowland?

I was, but I didn't want to admit it, even to myself. So, taking a deep breath, I decided that, given how bad the storm was getting, it was time to stop being frightened of a place that hadn't really changed, except in my imagination, and I trudged into the darkness.

Immediately, the hairs on the back of my neck started to prickle, but I kept going.

And when I was halfway through to the other street, I heard a noise.

Just like Miss Giddings must've heard right before the man walking next to her had been murdered in cold blood.

CHAPTER 85

AS I STARTED TO RUN, CURSING MY OVERSIZE BOOTS, I TOSSED the papers to the wind so I could pump my arms.

Maybe I was screaming, too, which didn't drown out the sound of footsteps right on my heels and heavy breathing, like the person chasing me was also struggling.

"No!" I cried, my heart pounding and cold sweat pouring down my back. "No, don't . . ."

Then, arms flailing, I stumbled on something—right before everything went black.

CHAPTER 86

ISABEL, CAN YOU HEAR ME?"

I felt someone shake my arm gently, and heard my mother's terrified, if quiet, voice rousing me.

"I'm tired," I grumbled, turning my head away. But the movement sent a powerful jolt of pain through my skull. Even so, I could hardly manage to move or cry out, and I weakly mewed, "Ow . . ."

I wanted to know where I was and what the heck had happened to me. It felt as if my head were wrapped in a turban, like I was Rudolph Valentino in his famous movie *The Sheik*. But I was mainly desperate to keep sleeping.

Probably the only thing that could've made my eyes pop open right then was hearing my mother growl, in a tone I'd never heard before, at somebody else in the room. "You . . . you had something to do with this, didn't you?"

CHAPTER 87

"MAUDE, WHAT ARE YOU DOING HERE?" I ASKED, CONFUSED. "And why is Mom mad at you?"

Maude, who was uncharacteristically pale, opened her mouth to speak, but my mother interrupted, squeezing my arm. "Just rest, Isabel," she urged. "Please."

With effort, I shifted to see that Mom wore her cleaning uniform, and I finally realized that I was in the hospital, where she should have been working, not sitting at my bedside.

Then my eyes, which had had been drifting shut again, suddenly opened wide when I caught a glimpse of Detective Culhane standing, arms crossed, at the foot of my bed. I recalled how he'd reminded me of the Grim Reaper the night I'd first met him, and I got a funny feeling in the pit of my stomach, as if he might actually have come to claim my soul.

I pulled my blanket up to my chin, only to notice Detective Hastings standing in a corner too.

"Hey," I greeted him, managing a weak smile.

"How are you feeling?" he asked, for once not getting silenced by Detective Culhane. "You okay, Isabel?"

"Not really," I admitted. Sitting up straighter, although that made the throbbing in my head worse, I looked around at the assembled adults. "What happened to me? Why are you all here?"

"That's what I want to know," Mom said, her voice low and angry. She was glaring at Maude, as if a certain famous reporter was responsible for me getting attacked in an alley. Fortunately — or maybe unfortunately — I was gradually remembering the events that had taken place . . . who knew how long ago. All I knew for sure was that I'd been walking in the dark, then running, then . . . clunk. "What is going on here?" Mom demanded. "Why is my daughter injured? Who did this?"

"Mrs. Feeney . . ." Maude was close to stammering, and she didn't have her notebook out. She turned to Detective Culhane, her eyes pleading. "James . . ."

"Believe me, Mrs. Feeney," Detective Culhane said with much more confidence. "I fully intend to find out who harmed Isabel."

I dared to look at him again, and although he was frowning, he seemed more worried than angry. Less like someone ready to snatch my soul and more like a concerned father. That was when I realized that I hadn't been *murdered*, so why was the Homicide Division involved?

Rubbing my head, which was covered by a big bandage, not a turban, I looked between Detectives Culhane and Hastings. "I didn't get killed," I pointed out. "So why did *you* come?"

"What happened to you might very well be related to a homicide," Detective Culhane informed me.

"But you said the killer is already caught," I reminded him. "You're *sure* it was Miss Giddings."

It had taken me less than a minute to make *him* want to bonk me on the head, but he held his temper in check —because he'd grown fond of me, in his own gruff way. I could tell. "You rest your brain, Miss Feeney," he suggested. "Let Hastings and me take care of investigating —as I've urged you, several times."

"What if I might have some ideas . . ."

There was warning in Detective Culhane's voice. "Isabel, I just told you . . ."

Maude intervened on my behalf. "James, perhaps you should listen to her. You need to hear Izzie's story at some point."

"Her *story*," he clarified. "Not her theories—"

"I told you, Albert Rowland threatened me," I said, talking over him. He *needed* to listen to me. "And then Aunt Johnene, when I sneaked into her boarding house looking for the gun—"

"What are you talking about, Isabel?" my mother interrupted, sounding even more alarmed. "A *gun?*" She addressed Detective Culhane. "Why does my daughter know a reporter *and* two police officers? Why is she talking about *guns?*"

"Mrs. Feeney . . ." Maude had regained her composure, and her voice was soothing as she moved closer to the bed. The contrast between the two women was striking. My mother's frizzy, graying hair and cheap hospital-issued dress paled even more than usual in comparison with Maude's smart skirt and silk blouse, her glossy black bob, and a pair of bright red pumps. Maude was tall to begin with and she loomed even larger given that my mother was sitting. Maude met my gaze for a moment, as if she was asking permission to explain, and I nodded because I knew she'd do a better job than I could.

"One of Isabel's regular customers, Colette Giddings, was at the scene of a shooting a few weeks ago—not far from where Izzie was selling papers," Maude told Mom. "Your daughter—very bravely—ran to help, although it was too late. A man, Charles Bessemer, was killed."

My mother's fingers tightened on my arm, and she gave me a sharp, apprehensive glance but let Maude continue.

"Miss Giddings is about to be tried for the crime, but Isabel has loyally defended her in spite of *my* doubts, which I have expressed in a series of newspaper articles. Izzie has been investigating too—apparently more than any of us knew." Maude smiled at me, just for a second, and I knew she admired how I'd tried to find the gun. Then she turned back to my mother. "You should be very proud of Isabel, for it seems that—given the evening's events—perhaps she's been correct about Miss Giddings's innocence."

Had I just heard right? Or had the blow to my head messed up my hearing?

"I . . . I don't understand," Mom said, still clinging protectively to my arm. "Are you saying—"

"It's possible that someone else did kill Charles Bessemer," Detective Culhane explained. "Because it seems odd that Miss Giddings is in custody but someone is still committing violence in that alley." He *finally* asked for my recollection of the events that had landed me in the hospital. "Isabel, what exactly happened?"

I rubbed my head again, trying to remember details. "I decided to go through the alley to return my unsold papers because I didn't want to be a coward. But halfway through, I heard something move—just like Miss Giddings said happened to her." My heart began to race, as if I were being chased again. "I started to run, but my stupid boots were so big . . ." I suddenly recalled something. "The person chasing me had trouble running too. I heard someone breathing really hard, and I thought I might even get away. But I tripped, and the next thing I knew, my arm was being yanked and twisted, hard enough to pull me back. Then . . ." I lightly rapped my head, which was a mistake, and concluded flatly, "Thunk."

"Fortunately, that skull is apparently uncrackable," Detective Culhane noted.

"James!" Maude spoke sharply, but her eyes twinkled.

Hastings coughed into his hand, stifling a guilty chuckle too.

My mother, who was not accustomed to potential homicides, especially ones involving her daughter, was not laughing, and Detective Culhane must've seen the disbelief on her face. "Sorry," he told her. Then he addressed me again. "Is there anything else you can recall, Isabel? Anything you heard or saw?"

"I didn't see anything, really. I sure as heck wasn't going to look over my shoulder!" My cheeks flushed. "And once I started screaming, I hardly heard anything else."

"Your screams saved you," Hastings reassured me in his kind way. "Somebody heard you and called the police."

That did make me feel better. I'd been getting embarrassed, looking back on how I'd shrieked like a baby.

"Is that it, Isabel?" Detective Culhane asked. "You can't tell me more?"

"Just that I *was* threatened by Aunt Johnene and Albert Rowland. Aunt Johnene said *I* might end up dead in an alley if I kept sticking my nose where it didn't belong."

My mother gasped, and Detective Culhane and

Maude shared a look that said, for once, both of them were taking me seriously. "I'll look into it," Detective Culhane promised.

"I think that's it," I said, wanting to close my eyes and rest again. All at once, though, I remembered something. Not anything I'd seen or heard, but something I'd *smelled*. I didn't know if it was important, but I added, "There was a funny stink, too, right before I got knocked out."

At some point Maude had pulled out her trusty notebook, but she stopped writing, clearly intrigued. "A stink?"

"Yeah," I said. "It was odd, but familiar . . . I was gulping for air, and I smelled it . . ."

Detective Culhane was waiting, his arms crossed again, and I struggled to remember more. But my head was really starting to ache. "Sorry," I finally said, shrugging. "The last couple of seconds, right before I got hit, are kind of a blur."

"Izzie . . ." My mother's face was ashen. "This is all so much . . . I don't know whether to be angry at you for getting mixed up in a murder, or proud of you, or . . . or just sick to think that I didn't even know what you've been up to while three other adults were well aware. And to think what *could* have happened . . ."

I didn't know what to say or do. The hurt in her expression, as she grasped just how incredibly removed she was from my whole life, rendered me silent. And

she was jealous, too, of my relationship with the educated, independent, commanding reporter who knew
more about me than she did. I could see it all in her
tired eyes. "Mom . . ."

Thankfully, Maude spoke up. "Isabel didn't want to
worry you. She kept everything quiet to protect you."

"She shouldn't have to protect me," Mom said
softly, bowing her head. "*I* should protect Isabel. And I
haven't—"

"Mom, it's okay," I said. "I work days, you work
nights . . ."

That wasn't helping, but my mother raised her face
and squared her shoulders. "Well, at least I know what's
going on now." She addressed Detectives Culhane and
Hastings. "And I promise you that Isabel won't have anything more to do with your murder investigation."

"And you *will* be investigating, right?" I asked Detective Culhane. "Because if you think there's a chance Miss
Giddings isn't the killer . . ."

"I will talk with Johnene Giddings and get to the bottom of the crime against you," he assured me. "But *Colette* Giddings's trial starts in one hour, and there is still
quite a bit of evidence that could convict her."

I jerked upright, which sent an arrow of pain shooting through my skull. "One hour?" I asked. "Really? It's
morning?"

"Yes," Maude confirmed, checking her wristwatch.
"I'm headed to the courthouse now."

"Izzie!" my mother cried as I swung my legs out from under the sheets without even thinking about what I might — or might not be — wearing, with two men in the room. Luckily, it was my usual pants and shirt. Mom grabbed my shoulder. "What are you —"

"I gotta testify!" I informed her. Then, although I knew it might hurt my mother more and put a friend in a very difficult position, I needed to do the right thing by Miss Giddings, whose life was at stake, and I begged Maude, "Please! Take me with you!"

CHAPTER 88

T HERE IS NO WAY MY DAUGHTER IS TESTIFYING AT A MURDER trial," my mother objected, rising, as if she were going to physically stop Maude from taking me. Not that Maude had volunteered yet. Mom appealed to the detectives. "She's already been injured as a result of this mess!"

"I understand your concern," Detective Culhane sympathized. "But we don't know for certain that the crimes are related, and Isabel *was* at the scene of the murder. She is a key witness."

It didn't help to remind my mother that before I'd been attacked, I'd nearly seen a homicide. Mom squeezed my arm again, more tightly than before. "She's not going anywhere."

I tried to shake free and bend to get my boots, which were peeking out from under the bed. She held me in place, though. "Mom, let go . . ."

Maude cleared her throat, so we all looked to her. "Mrs. Feeney, if I might say something?"

My mother didn't give any indication that she was eager to hear a reporter's two cents, but Maude continued in her calm, convincing way. "I've covered dozens—literally dozens—of murder cases just like this one . . ."

Wow.

"And the evidence against Isabel's friend is fairly substantial. I might not be convinced that Colette Giddings is innocent, yet. But Isabel has consistently raised doubts in my mind. Made me wonder if perhaps Miss Giddings *isn't* the killer. Izzie merely wants the opportunity to convince a jury, too, and possibly save her friend from the gallows."

My mom was a nice person. Probably too nice, which is why the world knocked her around so hard. But at that moment she stood up to one of Chicago's most powerful women, reminding Maude Collier that while she might have been a big-shot journalist, there was one key position Maude could never hold. "You are not Isabel's mother," Mom said evenly. "*Not* her mother. And you don't know what's best for her."

Maude's cheeks reddened, and I thought she avoided looking at Detective Culhane, who probably wanted kids that Maude couldn't have without giving up everything else. Still, Maude didn't completely lose her composure.

"I know that I'm not her mother," she agreed. "I was just trying to explain—"

"Or trying to get a good story." Mom cut Maude off. "Because surely a young girl testifying at a murder trial is a curiosity, right?"

My mother was savvier than I'd thought. But I told her, "Maude wouldn't use me like that."

"I promise you, I'm not looking for a story," Maude said. "I promise."

Mom crossed her arms over her chest. "Yet you had your notebook out a moment ago."

I couldn't believe how tough my mother was being, and I was suddenly very proud of her. Maybe she didn't have nice clothes or an expensive, fashionable haircut or a job that made her famous, but all at once, I really grasped how hard she worked to protect what was left of our family.

Yet I had a responsibility to Miss Giddings, and I knew that in her heart, my mother would want me to do the right thing. I tugged her arm, forcing her to listen to me. "Mom . . . a lady's life is at stake, and I know things that could help her." She wasn't convinced, and I added, "You've always taught me to 'do unto others.' And Dad *gave up his life* trying to protect other people."

I glanced at Detective Culhane, who had removed himself from the conversation, and saw that he was nonetheless listening intently, one hand rubbing his chin.

I really wondered what was going on behind his blue eyes, which didn't give away much.

If he were in my mother's place, would he react like a father, protectively, or like a soldier, and say I should do my duty?

I had a feeling it would be the latter.

"Mom." I tugged her arm again. "Dad would want me to go."

All at once, Hastings, whose presence I had nearly forgotten, spoke up from his corner. "She's trying to do right by her friend, Mrs. Feeney," he said quietly. "I think you should let her."

Mom turned to him and opened her mouth to protest one more time. Then her expression softened, and I knew I'd won. "I can't go with you," she told me, her voice taut with emotion. "I have to finish my shift before I can leave the hospital."

"Maude'll take me," I said without first asking the woman who I *did* believe was my friend, even if she would also feel obligated to put my story in the paper. Fortunately, Maude nodded, and I turned back to Mom. "I'll be okay."

"I'll watch out for Isabel too," Detective Culhane offered. "All she needs to do is answer a few questions today. I'll almost certainly be called upon to do the same, as I've done countless times before. It will be fine."

I had been assaulted in a dark alley, and my entire head

was wrapped in gauze, so my mother could have been forgiven for worrying that something might still happen to her only daughter. But even having money and a chauffeur and a bulletproof car couldn't guarantee anybody safety in Chicago, where gangsters often battled it out with machine guns on the street corners, hitting innocent bystanders, too.

Heck, let's face it. Nobody was safe *anywhere* from wars, or polio, or the influenza that had taken Detective Culhane's wife, or a million other terrible things. All most of us could do was go out the door every morning, do what we needed to do, and look out for each other as best we could.

"I'll be back in time to sell the evening edition," I promised my mother, hoping that was true. "Don't worry, okay?"

"Okay, Isabel." She forced the tiniest smile and, for the first time in a long while, smoothed my hair—except that my curls were hidden under a big bandage. Still, it felt nice. "Just watch what you say, all right? You don't always think before you speak."

I smiled too. She *did* still know me. Then I shot Detective Culhane a warning look, silently telling him not to agree about my big mouth, because I knew he was tempted.

"Come along," he said with a wave of his hand. "I'll drive you both to the courthouse."

"And I'll wait for you to finish your shift, Mrs. Feeney,"

Hastings volunteered. "Then I can take you home — or to the trial, if you'd like."

I realized, suddenly, that Hastings might have been quiet, but it wasn't necessarily because Detective Culhane was in charge. Hastings had his own important role to play, keeping people calm and helping them through the confusion and fear related to a murder investigation.

"Let's go, Isabel," Maude prompted. "We don't want to be late."

Crouching, I pulled on my boots, then followed Maude and Detective Culhane out the door. But before we got halfway down the corridor, I ran back and threw my arms around my mother. And for once I actually thought before I spoke, and I knew I said the right thing. "I love you, Mom."

Then I ran off, my head and my heart pounding, to have my say in court.

I just wished I was as confident as Maude and Detective Culhane about my safety, because something I couldn't quite put my finger on continued to bother me.

What had I smelled right before I'd blacked out?

And why did it worry me?

CHAPTER 89

THE TRIAL HAD ALREADY STARTED BY THE TIME WE GOT there, but Maude and Detective Culhane didn't seem worried about being late or concerned about the crowd, which was pretty big. I guess they'd attended plenty of hearings and knew their way around a courtroom. The uniformed bailiff who guarded the door, keeping out some folks who hadn't gotten seats, was obviously familiar with my escorts, too. As soon as we walked in, he nodded and said quietly, "Miss Collier. Detective. I can find spots for you."

"Isabel, here, is a witness, George," Maude noted, placing an arm around my shoulders.

Bailiff George nodded again, then crooked his finger, indicating that we should follow him. We walked right down the middle aisle, toward the judge, practically to the front. When we reached the third row, we all stopped, and George leaned down to have a quiet conversation with some folks who didn't seem too happy to have to stand up and leave. But I heard the bailiff tell them that if they didn't go at his urging, the judge would kick 'em out.

I mumbled "Sorry" to them, but Detective Culhane had his stone face on, and he placed one hand lightly on Maude's back, guiding her into the bench, then waved me in too. Apparently I didn't merit the more gentlemanly gesture.

Sitting down, I scooched over to make room for him, and when he was seated, I could finally pay attention to what was happening—which wasn't much. The judge was talking to the jury, telling them about their "obligations" and "reasonable doubts," so I looked around the courtroom, searching for familiar faces.

I quickly found Robert, who I wasn't sure would be there, and he gave me a funny look. It took me a second to realize that he was no doubt wondering why my head was all bandaged up. Since we couldn't talk, I shrugged and waved, and he offered me a small, sad, scared wave in reply. My heart sank, because even from across half a courtroom, I could see that he had that bluish tinge around his mouth, which concerned me for two reasons.

He was already in bad shape, and the day was just beginning.

And what if he distracted his mother, who would be worried about him?

Robert was sitting next to none other than Aunt Johnene, who was dressed like a schoolmarm in a prim, ruffled blouse and had the pursed-mouth, prissy expression to match.

Had she come hoping to watch her own sister get sentenced to hang?

And was she *not* surprised to see my injured head?

Or had she, maybe, expected that I wouldn't be there at all?

I couldn't tell. Then, glancing between aunt and nephew, I was struck by a bizarre possibility.

Would Aunt Johnene drag Robert to a trial on purpose, hoping to kill *him*? That little house she wanted to buy, if her sister was out of the way, would be a lot roomier without a sickly boy in it . . .

That theory seemed pretty far-fetched, but then again, Aunt Johnene was cold to the core. Cold enough that I honestly believed she might be responsible for the bump on my head.

I had the urge to stick out my tongue at her. But I was afraid she might also be a witness because of the gun, and it probably wouldn't help to make her more bitter and angry than she already was, so I turned away.

That was when I spotted somebody I'd never, ever expected to see at the trial.

Robert's father, Albert Rowland. He was dressed in a suit, as opposed to a bloodstained apron, and I could almost see why Miss Giddings had fallen for him. I was wearing a bandage turban, like Valentino in *The Sheik*, but Mr. Rowland actually bore a striking resemblance to the movie star who made every woman swoon.

As I studied him, I tried to figure out why he was there, then recalled how Miss Giddings said her husband had given her the missing gun. I also remembered how Detective Culhane had claimed that not all guns look alike.

Was Mr. Rowland a witness too? Would he take the stand to identify the weapon that had been found in the alley?

And if so, could he be trusted to be honest?

Because if he really hated Miss Giddings — or was the killer himself — he might have reason to fib . . .

Robert's father must've felt me staring at him. He shifted to look at me, and his eyes narrowed with recognition. *Unhappy* recognition.

Okay, maybe Miss Giddings shouldn't have fallen for a mean butcher, no matter how handsome he was. Albert Rowland might've had an alibi — at least one that Detective Culhane believed — but there was nothing kind in those dark eyes. I *still* thought he might've hurt me and killed Charles Bessemer, too.

I turned away first and looked straight ahead to where Miss Giddings sat, at a big table with the man I assumed was her lawyer.

Could I even call him a man, though? He looked more like a kid — a nervous child, playing dress-up in a suit with wide shoulders he didn't quite fill. Leaning close to Miss Giddings so they could confer quietly, he fidgeted with his necktie. Robert, who also wore a jacket and tie, looked almost as mature as Miss Giddings's defender.

I stole a peek at Detective Culhane, who sat stiffly next to me, his eyes trained on the judge, although he must've heard similar spiels a hundred times before.

Why couldn't somebody like him, who I might not always like but who definitely exuded confidence, be on the case *protecting* Miss Giddings?

I tapped Maude's arm, and she glanced down at me, whispering, "What, Isabel?"

"That lawyer looks awfully young," I observed. "Do you know him?"

"Yes, yes I do," she said.

"And . . ."

Maude frowned. "I'm . . . I'm sure he'll do his best."

That was all she said. It was all she needed to say. We both faced forward again, and I saw Miss Giddings nod at some comment by her incompetent attorney. She was hunched over, her body drowning in the pretty dress Flora had chosen. A few weeks earlier Miss Giddings would've had every man's attention in that frock, but now it hung on her skinny frame. And if she'd had her hair done, as Flora had suggested, it didn't show. Her curls were limp, the shade nearly as mousy as mine.

And speaking of Flora . . .

All at once I realized that somebody important was missing from the room.

A girl who seldom passed up a chance to be in the spotlight, even if it meant exploiting the fact that she was an orphan.

Just as I started to wonder if Flora Bessemer would actually skip the trial of her father's accused killer, maybe because she'd already found Miss Giddings innocent, the big double doors at the back of the room swung open wide, so everyone, including the judge, shifted to see a future film actress make her—of course—dramatic entrance.

CHAPTER 90

MISS!" THE BAILIFF CALLED, TRYING TO CATCH FLORA'S arm and stop her from entering the room, which was already beyond capacity. Detective Culhane, Maude, and I were squeezed into a spot that had previously been occupied by only two people. "Wait!"

Needless to say, Uncle Carl—part chauffeur, part bodyguard—wasn't going to let his "delicate" little charge get grabbed, and he stepped wordlessly between the bailiff and Flora, giving her a chance to tell the court officer, in her best "actress" voice, which just happened to project to everyone in the room, "Surely you can't deny *me* a seat at this trial! I'm Charles Bessemer's daughter!"

Most folks in the courtroom probably knew who Flora was, but it was such an exciting moment that a lot of people gasped at that revelation.

Heck, I gasped a little. It was like a scene from a play or a film.

Maude was scribbling too furiously to make a sound. She was also probably used to staying a bit detached from emotional moments so she could report them.

Could I ever achieve that?

And—I looked back at Flora—was she going to make this all about her, and not Miss Giddings? Because if the jury got all weepy for a pathetic orphan, they might be more likely to convict, just to get some kind of justice for the little Bakery Pride Bread girl, who continued to stand in the very center of the room, commanding attention like a miniature general in blue velvet, bows, and ribbons.

Flora didn't even pay attention to the judge—whose nameplate said THE HON. JOHN WAVERLY—when he banged a gavel and snapped, "Order! Order in this court!"

Nope. She just waited until the last echo of the gavel faded away, then said, firmly and clearly, "I am here to make sure that Colette Giddings goes free, because she did NOT kill my father!"

Talk about a huge gasp, and more gavel banging, and whispers that rose close to a roar—which made it difficult to hear the prosecuting attorney yelling, "Objection! Objection!"

Miss Giddings was twisting all around, her eyes wide, as if Flora's endorsement had alarmed more than pleased her, and her lawyer's jaw was flapping open too, which wasn't reassuring.

Meanwhile, on one side of me, Detective Culhane groaned and rubbed his forehead, while on the other side, Maude was grinning, no doubt at the prospect of landing on the front page with *this* spectacle.

And me—I was smiling too, as order was restored in the courtroom, the judge told everyone to ignore Flora's remarks, and the bailiff led Flora and Uncle Carl to even better seats than mine. Apparently, even if you messed up the whole trial, being the daughter of a dead man carried some weight.

One row ahead of me, a few feet away, Flora flounced into the bench, her curls bouncing, then leaned back past her uncle's massive shoulder so she could wink at me.

Yeah, Flora Bessemer might've been a self-centered pill, but she looked out for the people in her circle, and that made her okay by me.

We shared a conspiratorial grin, and then she turned around just in time for me to realize that the judge was directing the attorneys to make their opening statements. I started out listening closely to Miss Giddings's lawyer, but the room was warm, and he droned on for so long, seeming to say nothing, that even though I was worried, my aching head got the best of me and I began to nod off, bumping against Detective Culhane's arm.

In fact, I was dreaming about struggling down a dark alley, with my legs trapped in two huge polio braces, when I was abruptly awakened by Detective Culhane nudging me off his shoulder, Maude shaking me, and the sound of a man's deep voice intoning, "The prosecution calls its first witness."

Forcing my eyes to open, I groggily wondered who *that* unlucky person would be — only to hear the same man say, "Isabel Feeney!"

CHAPTER 91

I HAD RAISED MY SHAKY RIGHT HAND AND PROMISED ALL THE folks in the courtroom, the entire government of the United States of America, and God himself that I would tell the truth, the whole truth, and nothing but the truth about Charles Bessemer's murder—just as I'd fully intended to do even before I'd rested my left hand on a Bible. But when I actually sat in the big wooden seat next to the judge and looked out over the crowd while everybody stared back at me, I kind of forgot everything I'd found while investigating the crime.

Instead, I said all the wrong things every time the prosecuting attorney—a wiry man named Johnson—asked me the same questions a hundred different ways.

"So, Miss Feeney," he said, cleaning his tortiseshell spectacles with his handkerchief, "you say that when you arrived on the scene, the gun was right next to Miss Giddings?"

My curls were damp with sweat under my turban. "Yes, but—"

"It's a simple yes or no question," he reminded me, still rubbing his lenses with that stupid cotton square. He was no Clarence Darrow, but he was making me look like a fool. "A one-word answer will suffice."

I glanced at Flora, who had an *I told you so!* expression on her face. She'd warned me that I wouldn't get to say everything I wanted. Not that I could even remember what I'd planned to tell the jury.

Then I tried to wordlessly let Miss Giddings, who was struggling to keep her chin from quivering, know that I was sorry, right before I mumbled, "Yes."

Mr. Johnson leaned forward and cupped one hand behind his ear. "What's that, Miss Feeney? We need to make sure the court stenographer can hear. So please tell us again . . . Was the gun right beside Miss Giddings when you found her kneeling next to Charles Bessemer's corpse?"

I shouldn't have let my temper get the best of me, but I was sick of the way he was bullying me, and I balled up my fists and popped up onto my feet. "Yes!" I yelled, right into his face, at the top of my lungs. "Yes, it was!"

The gavel came swinging down, and Judge Waverly called for order in the court again, because lots of people were talking and some folks were laughing. I saw Detective Culhane lean over to confer with Maude, a smirk on

Johnene Giddings's face, and Robert . . . he looked like he
was *dying.* For a second, I stood frozen, forgetting about
the scene I'd caused and thinking I should tell somebody
to get an ambulance. But Robert could speak for himself,
and surely he knew how much he could handle. Besides,
the judge was addressing me. "Sit down, Miss Feeney,"
he said. "No more outbursts!"

I started to climb back into the big wooden chair,
promising myself that I would fix the mess I was making. But it was too late. "No more questions," Mr. Johnson said. "The witness is dismissed."

What?

"But . . . but . . ." I started to protest, only to have the
judge interrupt me.

"You are dismissed, Miss Feeney."

There was nothing I could do but step down, my
shoulders slumped in defeat, and drag my feet back to
my seat, purposely not looking at Miss Giddings, in case
she hated me—as she should.

"Please don't say anything," I mumbled, edging past
Detective Culhane. I fully expected him to make some
kind of remark about dumb kids. Therefore, I was very
surprised when he patted me on the back. "It's okay, Isabel," he whispered. "You did fine."

No, I hadn't, but I appreciated the reassurance—and
the way Maude squeezed my hand when I plopped down
next to her. "You honestly did well, Izzie," she promised,

leaning close. "Johnson came across as a bully. The jury was sympathetic to you."

I finally raised my eyes enough to meet hers. "Honest?"

She nodded, smiling. "Honest."

I looked warily at her notebook. "Are you gonna write about all this?"

"Of course. You've probably just earned yourself a spot on the front page!"

Having a famous reporter for a friend would likely always be challenging and a little confusing, but I no longer felt angry about being part of her stories. Maude genuinely cared about me too. "Don't forget, Izzie," she reminded me, "you'll get to say more when the *defense* calls you. That's when you can really speak up for Miss Giddings."

I'd forgotten that I'd probably have two chances to talk, and I felt better as I sat back to see how the next witness did.

But before anybody else could be called to the stand, Albert Rowland—whom I'd practically forgotten was there—stood up and said, "Excuse me, Your Honor. I think I need to take my son to a doctor. Now."

CHAPTER 92

"GOSH, I HOPE ROBERT IS OKAY," I SAID, LOOKING TOWARD the doors through which Albert Rowland had carried his son, who had been frighteningly limp. I met Flora's eyes again, just as both of us got jostled. We were in a crowded hallway outside the courtroom during a recess. Nobody was venturing too far, probably for fear of losing a seat when the trial reconvened. "He looked really bad, don't you think?" I added. "Like he was hardly breathing."

"He never looks great," Flora noted with a matter-of-fact shrug. "But yes, I'd say he needed a doctor."

"How strange that his father spoke up, after ignoring Robert for years—and abandoning him because he's sickly."

Flora'd been fixing her curls with the help of a mother-of-pearl mirror she'd pulled out of her little beaded bag, but she paused and frowned at me. "That really happened?"

"Yes. Mr. Rowland is terrible. Almost as bad as Robert's aunt!"

Flora resumed primping while I located Aunt Johnene, who *hadn't* gone to the hospital with her nephew. She was, for once, smiling sweetly—no doubt because she was chatting with the bailiff, who was young and not bad looking.

She wants to be married so desperately.

All at once, as I considered Robert's bad luck when it came to relatives, I had a terrible thought.

Is Robert safe with his father, who might be a pepsin-gum-chewing killer?

"Isabel! I'm talking to you!"

Flora nudged my arm hard with her elbow, which made my head hurt too. "Ow!"

"Sorry." She looked me up and down, from my bandage to my boots. "I keep forgetting that's not some unusual fashion choice on your part."

She was such a witch, yet I liked her.

"I was asking you to send me a letter," she said, snapping her bag shut. "To let me know how Robert's doing."

"What do you mean, send a letter?" I asked. Though it was nice that she cared about Robert, I didn't want to be her errand girl after the trial was over. "Just stop by and see him yourself."

She gave me a funny look. "How am I going to do that from California?"

"What?"

"I'm leaving, you know. For Hollywood," she reminded me, as if I'd forgotten she was going to be in a
movie.

Okay, maybe I had sort of forgotten that.

"You're really leaving?"

The news was surprisingly upsetting to me. It wasn't
that I'd thought Flora and I would spend a lot of time
together once we helped Miss Giddings get free, but I
didn't exactly want her moving to an entirely different
state, either.

Apparently that was happening, though. And soon.
"Yes," she informed me. "Uncle Carl and I are going by
train. Filming begins in less than a month." Flora beamed
with self-satisfaction. "We'll stay in an apartment building very close to the Pacific Ocean."

I narrowed my eyes at her, wondering if she was exaggerating, at least about the ocean. "Jeez, exactly how
much are they paying you to prance around onscreen?
Must be a lot!"

That was a terrible question and none of my business,
but Flora was more than happy to answer it—and the
number made my eyes pop. "Ten. Thousand. Dollars,"
she said, making sure to emphasize each word. "And I
already have an audition for another film, based on my
screen test." She fluffed her curls. "The executives at the
studio *really* liked me."

"I guess they did," I muttered, trying not to be jealous. I couldn't dream of making that much money if I sold *Tribs* every day for fifty years.

And that's probably just the start for her. She'll probably make loads of cash, because she is pretty, and has charisma, and can be cloyingly sweet when it suits her . . .

I was definitely teetering toward envy when Uncle Carl muscled his way over, his jowls flapping as usual, and took Flora's arm in his meaty paw. "Come on," he urged without so much as a "Hello, kid" to me. "Court's startin' up again."

Flora allowed herself to be led away but looked back over her shoulder. "I'll see you when this is all over, okay? And better luck if you testify again. I'm sure you won't make a mess of it the second time!"

I didn't respond. I was too busy thinking that if I, who actually knew Flora Bessemer, liked her, she almost certainly would become the nation's sweetheart when she turned on the charm for millions who wouldn't see her awful side.

Just how much money did she really stand to make?

And what was nagging at me right then, aside from my headache?

What was I not quite piecing together?

CHAPTER 93

AND MISS GIDDINGS'S FINGERPRINTS WERE ON THE GUN?" Mr. Johnson asked Detective Culhane, who was on the stand. "The gun found in the alley?"

Detective Culhane had no stake in whether Miss Giddings went free—probably still wanted her to at least go to prison, if not hang—and he wasn't fumbling or bumbling around with his answers.

"Yes," he confirmed with a slight nod.

If ever there was a person meant to respond with one word, it was Detective James Culhane.

Mr. Johnson rubbed his glasses and squinted. "Was she *holding* the gun when you arrived?"

"No."

We'd been going over all of this for what felt like hours, and even Miss Giddings appeared almost bored. Or maybe she was drooping even more to hear the facts laid out against her. Only Maude and some other reporters I'd noticed in the crowd—all men—continued to show sustained interest. But none of the male journalists' pencils flew as fast as Maude's. She took notes almost as rapidly as the stenographer typed.

I wanted to be a reporter too, and I knew I should practice paying attention, but my mind was definitely wandering far from the courtroom, if not the case.

A dark alley and a single gunshot.

Miss Giddings kneeling, her eyes wide and her coat stained with blood.

The smell of blood in a butcher shop . . .

I shifted in my seat, searching the courtroom, and was surprised to see that Albert Rowland had returned, although Robert was still missing. That had to be good news, right? Had to mean that Robert was safe and getting care in a hospital?

I studied Robert's father until he again felt my gaze and glared at me.

Or had Albert Rowland finally "disposed of" an inconvenient and embarrassingly weak child?

Shaking my head just slightly, dismissing that possibility as too absurd, I turned back around, letting my thoughts drift again, to Robert's house.

So warm and cozy—until Aunt Johnene arrived, smelling of mothballs and cabbage and desperation . . .

I probably should've stayed still, but I twisted to look at Johnene Giddings, too.

She was also preoccupied—watching the bailiff.

Really?

At your own sister's trial, while your nephew is maybe dangerously ill?

Although Aunt Johnene wouldn't see it, and a lot of other folks would probably wonder what I was doing, I gave in to the urge to stick my tongue out at her. Then I faced forward again, continuing to daydream, with the vague goal of putting together a puzzle that had a big missing piece.

The alley by daylight. Snow, disturbed on a doorstep. Chewing gum.

An abandoned building at night. A shadowy figure.

A fancy Italian restaurant where Mr. Bessemer ate—every Thursday.

Me, running.

Being grabbed.

A strange smell . . . again.

Flora Bessemer, about to be rich.

Blood.

Jealousy.

Siblings who might kill.

Inconvenient—and very convenient—children . . .

My heart was racing, and I still wasn't sure exactly what I was going to say when I jumped up off the bench just as someone in the courtroom, as if on a director's cue, *unwrapped a piece of gum.*

I probably should've whispered to Maude, giving her an exclusive, but as usual, I couldn't keep my mouth shut, and I ended up blurting out to everyone, my finger shaking as I pointed, "There! The real killer is right there!"

CHAPTER 94

UNCLE CARL COULDN'T RUN VERY WELL IN AN ALLEY, AND he definitely wasn't built for sprinting through crowded courtrooms. He thrashed like an enraged bull, trying to stumble out of the confining bench, trapped by folks who still didn't understand what was going on, even though I continued to explain at the top of my lungs, over the judge's calls for order.

"He killed his own brother so he could be Flora's legal guardian, because she's going to be a rich movie star!" I hollered. "He got sick of driving her around for pennies, when he could have control of the whole pot!"

Uncle Carl's face was beet red, and he continued to flail forward until he reached the end of the row and broke free, at which point I expected him to head for the hills, trailed by the bailiff, who had finally sprung to life.

Instead, though, Uncle Carl started stomping toward *me.* "That brat is lying!" he sputtered. "She's a lying little monster!"

"I am not!" I insisted as Maude finally dropped her notebook to put a protective arm around me. She and Detective Culhane, plus most everyone else in the courtroom, were standing up by then.

I caught a glimpse of Flora, who was fidgeting with her ribbons and bows, which had been disturbed when her uncle shoved past her. For once, her face was ashen. Yet she wasn't wide-eyed with complete surprise.

Did a tiny part of her suspect Uncle Carl because of the gum? Is that why she wouldn't let me mention it in front of him?

I didn't have time to wonder why a girl who'd vowed to avenge her father's death might've tried to protect her murdering uncle. Maude was stepping slightly in front of me, shielding me and urging, "Izzie . . . maybe you should run . . ."

Contrary to Flora's prediction, I would not be "shut up," though. I sidestepped Maude and resumed talking even faster, because the bailiff, who'd grabbed Uncle Carl's arm, couldn't hold him back forever.

"He chews pepsin gum all the time—even at his brother's funeral!" I cried, pointing again. "The kind of gum I found in the alley, stomped into a footprint in the snow. Only it smells awful on his breath because he also eats garlic constantly—at Napolitano's. He reeks of pepsin gum and garlic! I smelled it last night when he tried to kill me in the same alley!"

"You little . . ." Uncle Carl growled, lunging at me.

He'd dragged the bailiff close enough that I could get a whiff of his terrible breath again. "I shoulda finished you . . ."

I stopped yelling and looked right into Uncle Carl's evil, slitted eyes. "You knew your brother ate at Napolitano's every Thursday night. You knew he'd go through the alley. You sneaked through an empty building, waited there, and shot him."

Uncle Carl's shoulders heaved and his nostrils flared, making him look even more like a bull, but he couldn't quite charge. Not in a courtroom, with police and reporters and a judge watching the whole thing. But in his rage, he couldn't stop himself from basically confessing, either. "You just couldn't leave things alone," he snarled, his fingers flexing, as if he were about to strangle me. "I really shoulda cracked your skull wide open—"

Detective Culhane finally spoke up, calmly and firmly. "That'll be enough." Stepping down from the witness stand, he clapped one hand on Uncle Carl's big shoulder, and although Judge Waverly was technically in charge, Detective Culhane, as usual, acted like the real boss. "Bailiff—get the cuffs on him before he hurts Miss Feeney. Again."

Then Detective Culhane looked down at me and said the most surprising thing I'd heard during that trial. Or maybe during the course of my entire life.

"Good work, Isabel. Excellent detecting."

"Thanks," I told him. But I didn't want to be a police officer, and I turned to Maude—who was pale on my behalf but grinning at the prospect of a fantastic article —and asked, "Can *I* take a crack at writing this story?"

CHAPTER 95

NEWSGIRL'S OWN STORY OF COURTROOM CLASH

"Extra! Extra! I Solved a Murder!"

by Isabel Feeney

In the end, it was gum—g-u-M—not a gun, that spelled the end of the line for killer Carl Bessemer . . .

"Hey, kid, you gonna read that paper or sell it?"

"Yeah, yeah, just hold on," I said, folding the latest

edition of the *Trib* and handing it to a man in an overcoat. He gave me a few cents, which I tucked into my remaining good pocket. I was in a pretty happy mood, and as he walked away, I added, "Have a nice day!"

I hadn't written the main story about the trial and how Miss Giddings had been exonerated, but Maude had helped me get a small article into the paper. A piece called a sidebar, where I'd shared my personal account of how I'd solved the crime. And Maude believed I'd done really well. She especially liked my first line, about gum and guns, which would let Detective Culhane know I hadn't forgotten that he'd once assumed I couldn't even spell.

"That's what I meant when I told you to write an Isabel story," she'd said, beaming at me.

I could hardly believe I was a published journalist, and I had to resist the urge to peek at my article one more time. Even so, I found myself staring at the stack of papers at my feet, proud that a whole city would read my words.

"Isabel!"

I looked up to see that none other than Colette Giddings was calling to me as she hopped out of a taxicab. The sight of her waving and smiling reminded me of the terrible night Charles Bessemer had been shot. Except that Miss Giddings was thinner and still not as pretty as she used to be.

"Hey, Miss Giddings," I said, smiling but a little confused. "What are you doing here?"

"I wanted to say goodbye," she said. "And thank you."

I frowned. "Goodbye?"

"Yes," she confirmed. "Robert and I are leaving to-day. The doctor said he needs a warmer, drier climate, as soon as possible." Her cheeks flushed, and she looked toward the alley where so much trouble had started. "I need a change too," she said. "We're going to Arizona, where there's a clinic that specializes in treating children who've had polio."

I wanted to know how they could afford that without Charles Bessemer's money, but I couldn't ask. I supposed mothers found a way.

I was also curious about whether Aunt Johnene had ever admitted to having the gun Miss Giddings had given her, but I imagined that would always be a mystery too, since the pistol at the scene had turned out to be Uncle Carl's. Apparently he'd tossed it down after shooting his brother, hoping to make Miss Giddings look guilty.

"Tell Robert good luck," I said, trying to smile. In spite of getting my story in the paper, my heart suddenly felt really heavy to think that two of the three friends I'd made were leaving. "Tell him I hope he gets better."

"You can talk to him yourself," Miss Giddings said, pointing to the taxi. "He wants to say goodbye too."

I saw Robert's pale face peek out the window. He waved, and I dropped the papers I was holding and went over to say farewell.

CHAPTER 96

"ARE YOU SURE YOU'RE WELL ENOUGH TO TRAVEL?" I ASKED, leaning my head in through the taxi's window. "You looked pretty sick in the courtroom."

"Yeah, sick enough that my father helped me," Robert noted, breathing fairly steadily now that his mother was free and he didn't have a certain detective intimidating him all the time. It probably didn't hurt that he was getting away from Aunt Johnene, too. "Can you believe he was actually scared for me?"

"I kinda thought your dad might've been out to kill you," I admitted, with a glance over my shoulder to make sure Miss Giddings was out of earshot. She was standing at a polite distance—and staring toward the alley again. I looked back at Robert. "Really, I was a little worried that he might've had it in for you."

Robert wasn't surprised by that revelation. "It crossed my mind too. But he really did just want to get me to a hospital."

I hoped that my telling Albert Rowland that he was a poor excuse for a father had something to do with his actions in the courtroom, but I probably couldn't really take any credit. Still, I was glad I'd stood up for my friend back in that butcher shop.

"The whole thing was a pretty big adventure for a kid with a bum leg and a girl who sells newspapers, huh?" I said. "From the night I met you right up to you getting carried out of the trial!"

Robert offered me one of his rare smiles. "Yeah, I guess it was pretty exciting—now that it ended okay."

"What do you think's gonna happen with you and your dad?" I asked.

Robert shrugged. "I don't know. He said he'll write to me."

I didn't think Albert Rowland would ever be a great father, but I hoped he would at least try to do better.

"You could send *me* a letter," I suggested.

"As soon as I get settled," Robert promised.

All at once we didn't seem to know what to say, although there were dozens of things I would've liked to talk over with him. There just wasn't time. And I was kind of close to crying, too. I didn't like goodbyes.

"You ... you're coming back, right?" I ventured. "When you're better?"

Robert frowned and got quiet. "I'm not sure."

That meant no.

"Oh, well . . ." There was no sense in dragging it out. "I guess I better let you go. I need to sell my papers."

I started to withdraw my head from the cab, but Robert stopped me. "Hey, Izzie?"

I poked my nose back in. "Yeah?"

"Thanks for helping my mother—and for being my friend."

I was really getting choked up. "You too," I managed.

Then I turned around and gave Miss Giddings, who'd come closer, a quick hug.

A moment later they were both waving to me. And then they were gone.

I kept waving long after the cab had turned a corner, so I shouldn't have been surprised when someone asked, in a snooty voice, "What in the world are you doing, Isabel Feeney?"

CHAPTER 97

F LORA BESSEMER, YOU ARE STILL MEAN," I TOLD HER. THEN I remembered that she'd lost her father and that her uncle would almost certainly go to prison, if not worse —which was largely my fault. "But are you okay?"

"Yes, I'm fine," she said, as if the question had been odd. "I wanted to find my father's true killer, and I did."

Actually, I'd done that.

"You must be upset, though. Maybe even with me?"

Flora jutted her chin. "No. It's all right. I wanted the truth."

The girl who'd wanted the truth was lying right then. Flora wasn't fine, and things weren't okay. Still, I admired how she could put on a brave face, even if she came across as *too* tough sometimes.

"Why didn't you ever say anything about your uncle chewing the gum?" I asked. "You knew that might be important, right?"

"No," Flora said. "I didn't *really* think so."

"But you tried to shut me up every time I started to mention pepsin gum in front of him!"

"I just knew Uncle Carl chewed it, and I didn't want him to think you suspected him." She glanced at my head, which was still bandaged under my cap. "He — obviously — would silence anyone who even came close to blaming him for a murder. And you made such a big deal out of knowing the police and a reporter!"

I could hardly believe she was accusing *me* of bragging, but I didn't bother arguing about it. I was more interested in the kind thing she'd done for me. "So you were looking out for *me?*"

"Yes, I suppose so." She acted like it was no big deal. Then Flora's eyes clouded with genuine sadness. "Right up until you confronted him, I couldn't honestly believe Uncle Carl would be involved. Family *protects* family. It seemed impossible that he'd break that code."

What a strange clan those Bessemers were. I would never understand their complicated rules and relationships.

"I guess the movie's off, huh?" I noted. "I guess you're stuck here for a while."

"No." She frowned. "I told you, I'm leaving for Hollywood today."

I noticed then that she was wearing a car coat and a cute wool hat, a good outfit for traveling. "So . . . you're really still going?"

"Yes, of course!" She gestured to an automobile

waiting by the curb. "My Uncle Edwin is taking me to the train station now. Once in California, I'll be under the care of a 'hired representative' of the studio until more permanent arrangements can be made."

First of all, she had more uncles? Good luck with that!

And second, why was I so disappointed?

"Well, I hope you have lots of success," I told her. "If I ever have two cents to spare, I'll go see one of your films."

"Here." Flora was undoing the clasp on a new little clutch. "Let me—"

"No!" I protested.

Would she never understand that I didn't want her charity?

But Flora wasn't exactly giving me a handout. "I'm just trying to buy half a dozen papers, so I can take one and you can have lots of copies of your article, which I understand is very good."

She'd just offered me the first compliment of our friendship, and I decided to accept both the cash and the kind words graciously. Especially since I really wanted to keep a few clippings of my story. "Thanks," I said, holding out my hand. "That's real nice of you."

Flora piled coins onto my palm. More than were needed. She took one *Tribune* and folded it. "See you around, Isabel."

Flora and I weren't going to have a tearful goodbye.

We weren't like that. But I would miss her. "See ya, Flora. Take care."

She sashayed off, and a new—not quite as large—uncle emerged from the sedan and opened the door for her.

Really, Flora, good luck!

Then I returned to my pile of *Tribs*, setting aside five for myself before picking up an armful. It was nearly nine a.m., and the last few folks running late for work might want to buy a paper. I checked the boldest headline to see which story I should try to sell, because my sidebar wasn't exactly big news.

And of course, the top story was no real surprise. Two bootleggers had been killed in a rough neighborhood known as Back of the Yards.

I wondered, briefly, if Detective Culhane—and Hastings—were investigating. If so, I hoped Hastings would tell me all about it. He'd kind of taken a shine to my mother when he'd driven her home from the hospital. Mom tried to act as if she was hardly interested, but he was coming over for dinner the next time she had a night off.

Hastings wasn't exactly handsome or rich, but I could think of a lot worse men who could be courting my mom. In fact, the thought of her finding somebody as nice as the guy who'd once offered to carry Robert Giddings made me pretty happy.

And I felt even better when two people I *had* been

expecting rounded a corner, walking in my direction. They weren't hand in hand—but they would be. Detective James Culhane *wasn't* a coward, and—let's face it—Maude Collier was special. As they approached me, he was looking down at her with something very close to a smile on his face.

"Miss Feeney," Detective Culhane greeted me. "How's that hard head feeling today?"

Yeah, he was starting to like me.

"I'm doing fine," I told him. I looked up at Maude. "I just gotta sell a few more papers, okay?"

Then we would be off for an egg cream. I wasn't going to turn down the offer this time. I'd earned a reward by saving Miss Giddings and putting Carl Bessemer behind bars.

"Let me help you," Maude said, bending to pick up some papers. She winked at me and joked, "I'm pretty good at selling *Trib*s, you know."

Yeah, she was. And I wasn't doing so badly either. My name was right there next to hers, and I couldn't help feeling really proud when she raised up a copy, urging passersby, "Read all about the newsgirl who solved the murder! In her own words!"

Historical Note

THIS NOVEL WAS INSPIRED BY THE LIVES OF FIVE REAL women who covered crime for the *Chicago Tribune* during the 1920s. In particular, the character of Maude Collier is based on the *Tribune*'s star reporter, Genevieve Forbes Herrick, whose byline dominated the front pages throughout the decade.

For women to cover anything but cooking, fashion, and other news considered "suitable" for ladies was rare at that time, and in a city that was infamous for its violence, Forbes Herrick broke new ground for subsequent generations of female journalists by reporting on crime shoulder to shoulder with men.

Murderess's Row was a real place—a wing of the Cook County Jail set aside to house the many women accused of killing men during what was called "the heyday of the murderess" in Chicago. Forbes Herrick frequently covered homicides similar to the one described in this book and was a regular visitor to the jail. She also lamented, in print, that women used the jail as if it were a beauty salon, and that the pretty killers always went free, no matter how much the evidence pointed toward guilt. (The story of Sabella Nitti, related in the novel, is true.)

The work of the *Tribune*'s female crime reporters — Forbes Herrick, Maurine Watkins, Kathleen McLaughlin, Leola Allard, and Maureen McKernan — is largely forgotten today, but these women almost certainly inspired girls like the fictional Isabel Feeney to become journalists.